ALSO BY CLAUDIA MILLS

Dinah Forever

Losers, Inc.

Standing Up to Mr. O.

You're a Brave Man, Julius Zimmerman

Lizzie at Last

by Claudia Mills

SCHOLASTIC INC.
New York Toronto London Auckland Sydney
Mexico City New Delhi Hong Kong Buenos Aires

ISBN 0-439-46082-4

Published by Scholastic Inc., 557 Broadway, New York, NY 10012,
by arrangement with Hyperion Books for Children,
an imprint of Disney Children's Book Group, LLC.
SCHOLASTIC and associated logos are trademarks and/or
registered trademarks of Scholastic Inc.

12 11 10 9 8 7 6 5 4 3   2 3 4 5 6 7/0

Printed in the U.S.A.   40

First Scholastic printing, September 2002

For the girl I used to be

Lizzie
at Last

One

YOUR HOROSCOPE FOR MONDAY, AUGUST 25
Aries (March 21–April 19). This is a crucial day for you.
Decisions made today will affect you for many months. Be
bold rather than cautious. You have less to lose than you think.

Lizzie Archer lay in the backyard hammock, suspended between two ancient oak trees, and read those words for the tenth time as the late-afternoon shadows lengthened across the Archers' unmown lawn. During a lazy summer spent reading, writing, studying French, and playing her flute, Lizzie had started to look at her horoscope every day. It was such a poetic idea, that her life here on earth was affected in some mysterious way by the movements of distant planets and stars.

And how could she not believe in astrology at least a little bit when those very words appeared in her horoscope book as the prediction for tomorrow, the first day of seventh grade? If the first day of seventh grade wasn't a crucial day for her, what was? Decisions made on the first day of seventh grade would affect her for the rest of the year, maybe for the rest of her life.

Be bold rather than cautious. That applied, too. Lizzie didn't like climbing ropes in gym class, or swimming in the deep end of a pool, or playing sports. On the other hand, she wasn't afraid to be different from the other kids at school. She was the only one who wrote poetry, and she was better at math than all the others, and she dressed the way she wanted to dress, in clothes she bought at thrift shops rather than at the mall. That afternoon she was wearing one of her favorites, its long, flowing skirt filling the hammock with billows of fabric.

But that was just the problem. Lizzie was *too* different. "The Lizard," people called her. "The Brain." Oh, if only summer didn't have to end, the sweet, dreamy summer when she could lie in her hammock scribbling poetry, far away from the snide giggles and sarcastic remarks of the popular girls. Seventh grade was bound to be the worst year yet. In seventh grade, unlike sixth grade, there would be a dance, where Lizzie would be the only one who didn't go—or, if she went, the only one who didn't dance. She could already hear all the popular girls whispering about it, for weeks on end, in their cruel little cliques.

Lizzie turned back to her horoscope: *You have less to*

lose than you think. The line was a puzzling one. Lizzie knew she didn't really have anything left to lose in seventh grade, as far as the others were concerned. In their view, if you weren't popular, you didn't exist, except as someone to giggle about when they walked by you in the halls. Maybe the horoscope was trying, in its own cryptic fashion, to show her some way in which—in their eyes? in her own?—she could win.

She dropped the horoscope book onto the long grass beneath the hammock. From beside her, Lizzie pulled out her poetry book, covered in a pattern of purple pansies. She turned to a fresh page and wrote:

> *Be bold rather than cautious.*
> *You have less to lose than you think.*

Then she let the hammock sway gently as she searched for how to continue:

> *The shadows that surround you*
> *Will vanish if you blink.*
> *A new day for you is dawning.*
> *You stand upon the brink.*

She gave the poem a title: "Lines Written on Contemplating My Horoscope for the First Day of Seventh Grade."

A new day for you is dawning. You stand upon the brink.
Lizzie's new life was about to begin. If only she had a
clue to how to begin it.

Wandering inside the house later, she found her
mother and Aunt Elspeth in the kitchen. They were sis-
ters, and both had the same wild, curly red hair that had
been passed on to Lizzie. But Aunt Elspeth was in all
other ways as different as she could be from both of
Lizzie's parents. Lizzie's mother was a professor of English literature, doing research on Jane Austen: Lizzie
was named after the heroine of a Jane Austen novel,
Elizabeth Bennet in *Pride and Prejudice*. Lizzie's father
was a professor of philosophy, doing research on the nature of time. Both of them worked at home during the
summer, reading and writing for hours on end, lost to
the world, just like Lizzie.

Aunt Elspeth was the practical one in the family. She
was a mechanical engineer, recently divorced. Already,
after the first week of her two-week visit, Lizzie felt as if
Aunt Elspeth were a permanent member of their family.

"Lizzie, my love," her mother greeted her. With one
hand, she reached out to touch Lizzie's cheek; with the
other, she held open a book, from which she had been
reading aloud to Aunt Elspeth. Lizzie could see the title:
Collected Poems of W. B. Yeats.

Aunt Elspeth stopped stirring the spaghetti sauce

long enough to hold out a spoonful for Lizzie to taste. "Yum," Lizzie said. The meals had gotten better since Aunt Elspeth came. She didn't forget ingredients, the way Lizzie's parents did.

"Are you all ready for school tomorrow?" Lizzie's mother asked.

"I think so." Lizzie had had all her new school supplies for weeks. She loved buying school supplies. She could hardly look at a brand-new notebook or packet of binder paper without seeing an invitation to cover those empty pages with poetry. But she would feel more ready for school if she didn't know that giggles and stares and mean remarks were lying in store for her. Marcia Faitak had had all summer to think up new tricks to play on Lizzie, and all the other kids were probably waiting to laugh at her afterward.

"What are you going to wear?" Aunt Elspeth asked. "When I was in school, that was the big question: what you would wear on the first day of school, and what all the other kids would be—" Aunt Elspeth broke off, as if suddenly aware of Lizzie's ankle-length Victorian dress, unlikely to be the current fashion in West Creek. "Though I doubt you're as superficial as I was at your age."

"Lizzie!" her mother said then, snapping her book shut. "We forgot to get you new shoes."

Lizzie looked down at her bare feet. Her last

year's school shoes were too small, and her sandals had a broken strap. It was typical of Lizzie's family that school supplies had been bought weeks in advance, while shoes had been forgotten until the day before school began. Lizzie could just see herself limping into West Creek Middle School on the first day of seventh grade with her sandal strap dragging on the floor behind her.

"The sauce will be all the better for simmering awhile," Aunt Elspeth said in her brisk, decisive way. "I'll run Lizzie over to the mall before it closes, and we'll get her some shoes and any other last-minute things she thinks of. Just wear your sandals, honey. You can shuffle along from the car to the shoe store."

Aunt Elspeth already had her car keys out. She didn't have to spend ten minutes looking for them, the way Lizzie's mother did. "Ready, Mizz Lizz?"

Lizzie followed Aunt Elspeth to the car, still thinking about her horoscope. Shuffling along in a broken sandal certainly didn't make her feel very bold.

The mall was crowded, but under Aunt Elspeth's capable direction, Lizzie had new shoes in twenty minutes. Not just any new shoes, either, but shoes she loved—low, flat, ballet-type shoes that were almost as comfortable as going barefoot on soft spring grass.

Then, as she was leaving the shoe store, Lizzie saw

Ethan Winfield, with his mother. She froze, overcome with paralyzing shyness mingled with the thrill of seeing him again.

"What's the matter?" Aunt Elspeth asked.

"Nothing," Lizzie whispered.

She hadn't seen Ethan for almost six weeks, since the summer French class they had taken together had ended in mid-July. He had gotten a back-to-school haircut. The blond cowlick Lizzie loved so much had been partially tamed. It looked as if Ethan had grown an inch or two over the summer, but he would still be one of the shortest boys in the class, just as Lizzie would be the shortest girl.

"Do you know that boy?" Aunt Elspeth asked in a low voice.

Lizzie nodded mutely.

"Do you have a crush on him?"

Lizzie felt herself blushing until her cheeks flamed as red as her hair.

"Why don't you say something to him? Ask him what he's taking this year, how his summer was. Come on, Lizzie, be bold!"

Bold. Had Aunt Elspeth read her horoscope? Surely Lizzie had been bold enough in the past, writing poems to Ethan, even giving him one on Valentine's Day. Lizzie's all-too-obvious crush on Ethan was one of the many things the other kids teased her about. Where

Ethan was concerned, her horoscope should have said, *Now is the time to be cautious.*

Aunt Elspeth grabbed Lizzie's hand and hurried her forward to overtake the Winfields. Lizzie was side by side with Ethan. It would be rude not to say *something.*

"Hi, Ethan," Lizzie said softly. Oh, there were so many things Lizzie loved about Ethan: how he stood up for her in front of the others; how one time, the best time, he had taught her to light the bunsen burner in science class, after Alex Ryan had teased her for being afraid to strike a match. Ethan even liked reading, or at least Lizzie thought he did. He had done one of his sixth-grade book reports on *A Tale of Two Cities*, a longer book than anyone but Lizzie would pick to read.

Ethan looked embarrassed. Lizzie liked boys who were shy around girls, not like loud, bullying, wisecracking Alex.

"Hi, Lizzie," Ethan said. Lizzie loved hearing him say her name.

"Are you also out doing last-minute school shopping?" Aunt Elspeth said to Ethan's mother, as if the two of them were old friends.

"I had no idea Ethan had grown so much over the summer. When I made him slip on a pair of his jeans this afternoon, there was a gap like *that*"—she held her fingers two inches apart—"between his pant leg and his ankle. And how he can go through a pair of tennis shoes in three months . . ."

As the two women continued to chat, Lizzie stole another glance at Ethan. If possible, he looked even more embarrassed than he had before. He couldn't be that uncomfortable just because his mother was talking about him to some strange lady.

At that moment Lizzie realized they were being watched. She heard Marcia Faitak's familiar giggle, and then her squeal: "It's the Lizard! Talking to her lover boy!"

Another girl's voice—Lizzie refused to turn around to see whose it was—said, "Look at her *dress*. Should we tell her what century it is?"

Lizzie hated both of them then. She had thought she looked pretty and romantic in her long, flouncy, white cotton dress, which just skimmed her ankles. Wearing it, she had felt like someone in a poem. Now she felt funny-looking, different, like someone who would never fit in. No wonder Ethan Winfield couldn't bring himself to like her.

All the humiliations of sixth grade came flooding over her in a tidal wave of shameful memories. The worst, the cruelest, the one she could barely stand to let herself remember, was when Marcia had tricked her into sending a poem off to a fake contest, and then sent her a fake letter telling her she had won. Marcia had somehow

11

gotten Ethan to take part in it, too. Lizzie had been so proud and happy when the letter came—her first-ever publication! Then Ethan had broken the truth, that it had all been a joke, designed to make fun of her in the nastiest possible way just because she loved to write. At least Ethan had been brave enough, and kind enough, to try to make things right with her afterward. But Lizzie still couldn't look at Marcia or Alex without remembering.

Finally, Aunt Elspeth let Ethan's mother go. Lizzie and Ethan had stood silent through their whole conversation, Lizzie overcome with her painful memories, Ethan seemingly overcome with shame at being seen with Lizzie.

"I think he's cute, too," Aunt Elspeth said to Lizzie when the two of them were alone again. The jeering girls had moved on, shadowing Ethan. Apparently it was more fun to stalk a cute boy than a girl who wrote strange poems and wore funny clothes.

Aunt Elspeth hesitated. Then she said, "Those girls? Do you know them from school?"

Lizzie nodded miserably. She had been hoping that Aunt Elspeth was too absorbed in her own conversation to overhear their remarks, but she had heard everything.

Suddenly Lizzie couldn't bear starting seventh grade if seventh grade was going to be like sixth grade, another year of Marcia's giggles, of the other girls' shrill laughter, of Ethan's embarrassment, of the crushing loneliness of being the smart girl, the different girl, the one who didn't fit in. A lump of unshed tears swelled in her throat. With painful clarity, she knew exactly what the horoscope meant now.

"Aunt Elspeth? While we're here? You said, if there was anything else I needed . . . Well, I might . . . Do you think you could help me buy something new to wear on the first day of school? My mother'll pay you back later . . ."

"Look, honey," Aunt Elspeth said gently, "I don't have anyone to spend my money on since my divorce, and we came to the mall to get you what you need for school, so let's pop over to The Gap and buy you a few things. I love picking out clothes for people. Shopping is one of my talents."

An hour later, Lizzie and Aunt Elspeth each had a bulging bag full of jeans, tops, and sweaters. Lizzie hated to think how much money Aunt Elspeth had spent. But the clothes crammed into those two enormous shopping bags meant that Lizzie would start school tomorrow utterly transformed.

When she had seen herself in the three-way mirror in the dressing room, Lizzie had been shocked. She hadn't looked like the Lizard at all, but like any other girl, like Marcia and her friends, like a girl on the cover of a teen magazine. Like someone Ethan Winfield could like? Like someone he could dance with at a seventh-grade dance? Lizzie didn't know. She felt half-scared, half-excited, at the prospect of finding out. She would boldly enter seventh grade tomorrow as the new, improved Lizzie: Elizabeth Bennet Archer, normal seventh-grade girl.

You have less to lose than you think.

Two

No. Lizzie couldn't go through with it. She could hardly stand the thought of going down to breakfast dressed in her new clothes, let alone walking into West Creek Middle School. She could barely look at herself in the full-length mirror on the back of her bedroom door. But she did.

The straight-legged jeans felt stiff and awkward encasing Lizzie's slim legs. Lizzie never wore jeans. Until the shopping trip with Aunt Elspeth last night, she hadn't owned a single pair.

The skinny spaghetti straps of the tank top left Lizzie's white, freckled shoulders bare, and the turquoise shade seemed blinding. Lizzie never wore bright colors. She usually wore white, like Emily Dickinson, the nineteenth-century poet who wrote poems all day shut up inside her house in Amherst, Massachusetts. Emily Dickinson was famous as a recluse, someone who hardly ever left her house. Lizzie doubted that Emily Dickinson would have worn anything like this in her bedroom, still less out in public, even if she had lived in Lizzie's time.

Maybe the tank top was too much for the first day. Lizzie held up another of the tops Aunt Elspeth had picked out—a skimpy little green T-shirt. At least it would cover her shoulders and the tops of her arms.

"Lizzie!" her mother called up the stairs. "We're leaving in ten minutes!"

Lizzie tore off the tank top and tried on the T-shirt. She felt more comfortable in it, but not as comfortable as she would have in one of her antique white dresses.

"Lizzie!" Aunt Elspeth called this time.

But the point wasn't to be comfortable. The point was to make seventh grade as different as possible from sixth grade. Lizzie switched back to the tank top, hunching her shoulders to make sure the straps stayed up. Bold rather than cautious. That was the theme of the day, of the new school year, of the new Lizzie Archer.

When she made herself walk into the kitchen, her father was at the table reading his *New York Times*. It cost a ridiculous amount to have *The New York Times* delivered every morning to their house in West Creek, Colorado, but Lizzie's father couldn't start his day without it. Lizzie's mother had her back to Lizzie, slicing fruit for everyone's lunches. Aunt Elspeth looked up from her latte and smiled encouragingly.

Lizzie's mother, finished with the fruit, turned from the cutting board. For a moment she just stared. "Lizzie?"

Her father looked up from his paper. "There's a fascinating article here about Tajikistan," he said to Lizzie's mother. Lizzie knew that Tajikistan was a foreign country—somewhere in Asia? Certainly far away from West Creek Middle School in West Creek, Colorado. "I'll bring the paper back home with me this evening so you can have a chance to read it."

He went back to his paper, but Lizzie's mother still stood staring.

"It's my new look," Lizzie said, as if that weren't obvious.

"Elspeth, did you happen to do any other shopping at the mall last night when you bought Lizzie's shoes?"

Aunt Elspeth's eyes met Lizzie's. "We got a few things."

Lizzie suddenly felt defensive under her mother's gaze. "You don't like it," she said.

"I didn't say that. But you have to admit you look *different*, honey."

"I want to look different," Lizzie said, pouring milk on her cereal. Or, rather, she *didn't* want to look different.

She wanted to look different from the way she used to look, not different from the other girls.

Lizzie's parents dropped her off at school on their way to the university. As they pulled up to the curb, Lizzie thought again: *I can't do it.* She wished she had crammed one of her dresses into her backpack so she could run into the girls' room and change. But she hadn't.

"All right, Elizabeth, dear one." Her mother leaned over and gave Lizzie a kiss. From the backseat, her father laid down his paper long enough to give a gentle tug to one of her bright red curls. Lizzie wondered if other kids' parents kissed them and tugged at their curls before dropping them off. Was that something you were still allowed to let your parents do in seventh grade?

"I know you're going to do well this year, the way you always do," her mother said. "Seventh grade will be a breeze for you."

As if it were her *subjects* Lizzie was worried about. As if a person wearing a bright turquoise tank top for the first time was worried about how she would do in seventh-grade math and social studies!

Since she had no choice, Lizzie got out of the car. Her parents drove off, leaving her there.

Seventh grade had begun.

Lizzie joined the crowd milling around in front of the West Creek Middle School doors. For the first time she really looked at what the other girls were wearing. She saw a few short skirts and a fair number of shorts, but most were wearing jeans just like hers, with a variety of tops, some like the green T-shirt she hadn't worn, some like the turquoise tank she had on.

Three girls talking together shot a look Lizzie's way, then started to laugh. Were they laughing at Lizzie? Or at some private joke of their own?

Lizzie saw Alison Emory, who had been in her summer French class, too. Alison had been nice enough to Lizzie in French class, though Lizzie had spent class breaks writing in her notebook rather than trying to socialize. Lizzie vaguely remembered that Alison had hung around the year before with a quiet girl named Melissa, and that Melissa had moved away over the summer. In any case, Alison, like Lizzie, was standing by herself right then. Yes, Lizzie would practice on Alison before she had to confront Marcia, Alex . . . and Ethan.

"Hi, Alison."

Alison's eyes widened. "Lizzie?" It felt like a replay of the scene at breakfast, except that Alison was clearly *not* disapproving, and Lizzie still wasn't sure what her mother had thought about the startling change in her daughter. "You look great!"

"Thanks," Lizzie said, trembly inside with relief.

"I love that top! It's perfect with your hair."

Alison's top was almost exactly like Lizzie's, but orange instead of turquoise.

"I like yours, too," Lizzie said, though she couldn't figure out what there was to *like* about a small piece of bright-colored fabric with two little straps.

"What are you taking?" Alison asked.

Lizzie pulled out her schedule card, which had come in the mail a couple of weeks before. Alison pulled out hers, and they compared classes.

"I have first-period orchestra and second-period English, too," Alison said, sounding pleased. "And sixth-period family living."

Alison turned to greet some other friends Lizzie didn't know. Lizzie put her card away. Would Alison have acted happy about having classes together if Lizzie had been wearing one of her old dresses? Alison had never made fun of her, the way Marcia did, but she had never been particularly friendly, either, though maybe that was because she'd had a best friend of her own. Lizzie had never had a best friend; no other girl had ever wanted to be friends with Lizzie before. It suddenly occurred to Lizzie that the old Lizzie, the Lizard, had spent her entire childhood in the company of adults, or alone.

A sudden shaft of sadness struck Lizzie for the girl she used to be. She felt the familiar swell of a poem, stirring inside her.

For the Girl I Used to Be

You, there, in the white lace dress—
In the dress from long ago—
Standing there, all alone—
Don't you know?

You, there, from another time—
You, there, from another place—
Don't you know, girl in white lace,
You're all alone?

Lizzie shrugged off her backpack and unzipped it to take out her notebook. She had learned from experience that if you didn't write down a poem right away, it would disappear.

Then she stopped. It wasn't just her clothes that had made her different from the other girls. The other girls didn't sit down wherever they were, open their notebooks, and start scribbling poems. If she was going to fit in this year, if she wasn't going to be all alone for the rest of her whole, entire life, she was going to have to change more than just her clothes. She was going to have to study the popular girls, the girls like Marcia Faitak, and make herself do the things they did, and act the way they acted.

The bell rang. Lizzie rejoined the crowd that carried her up the stone steps into middle school.

In homeroom she turned over her schedule card and tried to jot down on the back as much as she could recall of the poem.

For the Girl I Used to Be

You, there, in the white lace dress—

She couldn't remember the rest. The poem was gone.

The person Lizzie wanted to compare schedules with was Ethan, but of course she couldn't. She just had to wait to see if she had him in any classes. He wasn't in first-period orchestra, but Lizzie hadn't expected him there; Ethan didn't play an instrument. What if he was in none of her classes? She pushed the thought away.

As soon as she took out her familiar flute, Lizzie forgot her unfamiliar clothes. She loved the feel of the slender silver instrument in her hands; she loved the sounds of its high, clear notes. She had practiced a lot over the summer—well, not really practiced, just played, sometimes for hours, until her fingers ached and her lips stiffened. Mr. Harrison looked impressed when Lizzie played a brief solo for him. She was proud to show him how much she had improved. Alison's clarinet was sounding lovely, too.

On the way to second-period English, Lizzie stopped

at her locker to put her flute away. Marcia was at her locker, a few doors down. Lizzie decided not to say anything to her. She wasn't feeling *that* bold. But she lingered a few extra seconds to give Marcia time to see her. She might as well get the first encounter over with, out of Ethan's hearing.

Marcia turned around. Like Lizzie's mother, like Alison, she stared.

Lizzie waited. She couldn't believe she cared so much about how Marcia would react to her new clothes. But she did.

"Well!" Marcia finally said. "Who dressed *you*?"

The tone was pretty mean, but not completely mean, not as mean as the tone Lizzie had overheard yesterday in the mall.

Lizzie took a chance. "Do I look all right?" she asked. After all, she couldn't very well pretend she had always dressed this way. As of yesterday afternoon, she hadn't. And no one knew that better than Marcia Faitak.

Marcia took a step back and squinted appraisingly at Lizzie. "Sure," she said with a shrug. Her dismissive tone added the words she didn't say: as if anybody cares what *you* look like. "It's better than looking like you're in some kind of time warp."

The last comment stung. But Lizzie decided to take Marcia's verdict as a positive one, anyway.

As she entered English class, Lizzie quickly scanned

the room for Ethan. He wasn't there. But then, as she was slipping into a vacant seat, she saw him coming through the door with his best friend, Julius. The two boys looked funny together, because Ethan was so short and Julius so tall. The only empty seats were in front of Lizzie and Marcia. Ethan and Julius took them without a backward glance.

The teacher, Ms. Singpurwalla, introduced herself. She was beautiful, with dark skin, dark hair, and dark eyes, and was dressed in a pale lavender sari. She spoke in a low, soft voice that held the class's attention better than a louder voice would have.

"Class, this year we're going to begin with a study of one of the plays of the great English playwright William Shakespeare. Have any of you ever seen a Shakespeare play performed on the stage?"

Had Lizzie ever seen a Shakespeare play? Ever since she was five years old, her parents had taken her each summer to an outdoor performance at the university's annual Shakespeare festival. There, as the twilight deepened to darkness and stars spread over the cloudless Colorado sky, she had sat between her mother and father and watched the magic unfold. *Romeo and Juliet, The Taming of the Shrew, As You Like It, The Merchant of Venice, Antony and Cleopatra, A Midsummer Night's Dream, Hamlet, Much Ado about Nothing*—she had seen them all.

She raised her hand. A few other people put up their hands, too. Not Ethan, not Julius, not Marcia.

Ms. Singpurwalla called on a dark-haired boy named Tom, who was sitting in the front row. Lizzie had never had him in a class before. "What have you seen?" Ms. Singpurwalla asked Tom.

"I saw *Romeo and Juliet* last summer at the Shakespeare festival," Tom said.

From the back of the room, Alex Ryan snorted. "Romeo, Romeo, wherefore art thou, Romeo?" he called out in a falsetto voice.

"Have you seen the play, too?" Ms. Singpurwalla asked Alex.

"Me?" he asked. "No." He made *no* sound like *no way.* "I heard that line once on TV. It was in a commercial. A dog food commercial."

Ms. Singpurwalla looked confused.

"They had this lady dressed up like Juliet, and she was standing on this balcony and saying, 'Romeo, Romeo, wherefore art thou, Romeo?' And then she put out this bowl of dog food, and this dog came running up and ate it, and she said, 'Good dog, Romeo.' "

"Oh," Ms. Singpurwalla said, her voice still low and pleasant. "Shakespeare's plays have had an enormous influence on our culture in many ways. What plays have the rest of you seen?"

One girl had seen a movie version of *Hamlet.* Another had acted out a scene from *Macbeth* in a summer drama camp. Beside Lizzie, Marcia giggled.

"What about you?" Ms. Singpurwalla asked Lizzie.

She had put her hand down when she saw that Marcia hadn't raised hers, but Ms. Singpurwalla must have noticed it. "I've seen . . ." She wasn't going to give the whole list. "I've seen some of them in the Shakespeare festival, too."

She could hear Marcia's little snort of contempt and tried to ignore it.

"Which one was your favorite?" Ms. Singpurwalla asked.

Lizzie tried to decide. The speeches in *Hamlet* were incredible, and *Much Ado about Nothing* was so funny, and the doomed lovers in *Antony and Cleopatra* had broken her heart. But the one she loved the very best was *A Midsummer Night's Dream.*

"A Midsummer Night's Dream," she said.

She was suddenly aware that Ethan had turned around to look at her. Did boys notice clothes the way girls did? Her father didn't, but Lizzie was aware that he was hardly typical of the boys in her class.

Lizzie met Ethan's eyes and held his gaze for a long moment. Then, blushing scarlet, he turned away.

He *had* noticed her clothes. She was almost sure of it.

"Well," Ms. Singpurwalla said, "it just so happens that *A Midsummer Night's Dream* is the play we're going to be studying this fall." She gave Lizzie a warm smile.

Lizzie smiled back, until she noticed how bored Marcia was looking with the entire discussion of who had seen which Shakespeare play. Maybe popular seventh-grade girls didn't smile at their teachers. She stopped smiling in the nick of time. Modeling herself after Marcia wasn't going to be easy: Lizzie could tell that already.

But she was still smiling inside. She had survived her new clothes. Alison had been friendly; Marcia had been considerably less mean; they were going to be reading *A Midsummer Night's Dream*; Ethan would be in class with her, and he'd blushed when their eyes had met. So far, so good.

Three

Lizzie was with Ethan in third-period math, too, and their teacher was Mr. Grotient, the same teacher they had had for sixth-grade math last year. As they walked into class, Ethan just ahead of Lizzie, Mr. Grotient greeted them both with a big smile. He was the only male teacher at West Creek Middle School who wore a suit—with a bow tie—and his plump body filled out his jacket and trousers like air in a balloon. Lizzie liked Mr. Grotient. He was a kind man and a good math teacher, *and* he had paired her with Ethan for Peer-Assisted Learning last spring.

"We'll be doing PAL again this year," he told the class as the students took their seats. "I want to keep last year's partners together, if I can, at least when they worked well as a team."

Ethan blushed for the second time that morning, and Lizzie felt the color rising in her own face. Peer-Assisted

Learning had worked out well for her and Ethan because she was good at math and Ethan wasn't. Or, rather, hadn't been. He had come a long way in a couple of months, thanks to Lizzie's patient tutoring.

The question suddenly occurred to Lizzie: Did boys like girls more or less when the girls helped them in math? She made a mental note to find out. Aunt Elspeth would probably know. As an engineer, she had to be awfully good in math. And she had gotten married, so she had to be good with boys, too. Of course, now she was divorced. Maybe Lizzie wouldn't ask Aunt Elspeth. This was the kind of thing Marcia would know. But Lizzie didn't think she would ever be brave enough to ask her.

To Lizzie's relief, Mr. Grotient didn't have them work with partners on the first day. The first day of seventh grade was intense enough without having her desk pushed up against Ethan's, their heads bent together over the same book.

Ethan wasn't with Lizzie in fourth-period social studies. She saw him at fifth-period lunch, with Julius, across the crowded cafeteria. She had brought her lunch from home and took it outside to a picnic table under a tall shade tree. The cafeteria was too small for West Creek's growing student body, so on nice days they were encouraged to eat outside. Lizzie sat alone, as usual. Her clothes certainly didn't cause a stampede of new friends to her table.

Alison came outside with some other girls; she didn't come over to sit with Lizzie, but she waved, and the wave made Lizzie feel more hopeful again. The soft late-summer breeze felt good on Lizzie's bare shoulders. For minutes at a time, she had found herself forgetting about her clothes. Maybe she'd get used to them one day.

Sixth-period family living was held in one of the specially designed rooms in the new wing of the school building. Lizzie's summer French class had used the kitchens there for French cooking. Family living was a requirement for all seventh graders, boys and girls.

The family-living teacher, Ms. Van Winkle, looked energetic and upbeat—sort of like Aunt Elspeth in the decisiveness of her movements. The room was filled with tables, each with six chairs. Lizzie sat down at the table closest to a window. It was one of her fixed principles always to sit near a window.

To her surprise, Alison hurried over to join her. "This is going to be the coolest class," Alison said. "I love sewing, don't you? And when we cook, we'll get to eat everything we make, and I've heard they fix some really yummy stuff."

Lizzie was about to say that she liked old-fashioned sewing, the kind you did with a needle and thread, not the kind you did on a sewing machine, when Marcia came in, Alex Ryan trailing behind her. Alex liked Marcia, Lizzie was almost sure of it. At least, he spent a disproportionate amount of time teasing her—not in the nasty way he sometimes teased Lizzie but in a playful, flirtatious way.

"Marcia! Come sit with us!" Alison called out in her friendly voice.

Lizzie stared at the ceiling, trying to pretend that she didn't care what Marcia would do next. Out of the corner of her eye, she saw Marcia survey their table, hesitate, then shrug. Like a queen, Marcia swept across the room and settled herself next to Alison. Lizzie let out her breath.

"I want the tables balanced, boys–girls," Ms. Van Winkle announced as students continued to arrive and look for places. The two girls who had been heading toward Marcia chose another table, leaving the three boy seats still vacant.

Sheepishly, Alex sat down next to Marcia. "But if we cook today, I'm not eating anything you help make," he told her. She swatted him, then giggled. Lizzie took note: boys like girls who swat them; boys like girls who giggle.

Then Ethan and Julius came in. Now Lizzie was sorry she had chosen the table by the window, farthest from the door. She couldn't very well expect Ethan to walk by all the other tables to sit with her. How could she even think that he might? Last year he would have gone out of his way to avoid sitting with her.

But Lizzie's was now the only table with two seats open. Would Ethan choose to sit with Julius even if it meant he also had to sit with Lizzie? He did. The two boys completed their table.

"Class!" Ms. Van Winkle clapped her hands; the emphatic gesture felt like a clash of cymbals, calling them all to attention. "Welcome to family living. West Creek Middle School's a big place, and I know we have a number of new students with us this year, so I want you to take a few minutes to introduce yourselves to everyone at your table. You're going to be members of the same family-living family for the rest of the year."

For the rest of the year? Marcia shot Lizzie a look that seemed to say: I was willing to sit with you for one *day*; I certainly didn't know I'd have to sit with you for the whole *year*. Ethan, too, had an expression on his face that Lizzie could well imagine on the faces of prisoners on death row.

"I've made up a little game to help you get to know one another better," Ms. Van Winkle went on. "I want you to find one thing that you all have in common, and then find one thing that is distinctive about each of you—some characteristic that no one else at your table shares. Everyone understand? All right!"

For a moment no one at Lizzie's table said anything. Then, as if making the best of a bad situation, Marcia took the lead. "Well, we all live in Colorado."

"That's not an interesting enough thing," Alison protested. "I mean, everyone in the whole *school* lives in Colorado."

"Were you all born in Colorado?" Ethan asked.

Lizzie, Marcia, and Julius were; Ethan, Alison, and Alex weren't.

"How about, do we all ski?" Alex asked.

The others nodded. It would have been easy enough for Lizzie to nod, too, but she couldn't honestly do it. "I don't," she said apologetically.

"Ride bikes?" Alex tried again.

Lizzie felt more embarrassed shaking her head this time.

"You don't ride a bike?" Alex asked, his tone scornful, unbelieving. "But you must know how to ride a bike."

Lizzie felt her face giving her away. She knew it was strange that she didn't know how to ride a bike, that she had never even tried to ride one, but that was the way it was. Her mother couldn't ride a bike, either. She felt like giving up. New clothes or no new clothes, she would never be like the others.

Luckily, Julius made another suggestion. "Do you all like pizza?"

"Actually," Alison said, "I don't. I hate anything with cheese on it."

"Ice cream?" Julius offered.

This time they all nodded, even Lizzie. Lizzie felt a

surge of relief. There *was* something she had in common with all the others, after all.

"Okay, then," Marcia said, resuming the leadership role. "Now something we don't have in common. I'll go first. I can do a split. Can any of you do a split?"

Nobody could.

"I do rock climbing. Do any of you rock-climb?" Alex asked.

Nobody did. Two down, four to go.

"I play the clarinet," Alison said. "Anybody else, clarinet?" The others shook their heads.

Lizzie had been afraid she would have to say something like, "I write poetry," or "I have a closet full of strange clothes." But Alison had made it easy for her. "Flute?" Lizzie asked. Sure enough, she was the only one who played the flute.

She waited to see what Ethan would offer.

"Umm . . ."

She could tell he couldn't think of anything. She knew he didn't play an instrument. He liked basketball, but so did Julius and Alex. He had read *A Tale of Two Cities*, but so had she. He was good in science, but she was good in science, too.

Julius spoke up. "Any of you ever change a diaper?"

Alex pretended to gag. Marcia squealed with disgust and horror.

"Ethan and I have. But we did it together."

"Then it doesn't count," Marcia said.

"We can't share it? It was a pretty major thing, let me tell you."

"No." Marcia held to her ruling.

"Okay," Julius said good-naturedly. "Have you ever been to Mesa Verde?"

Alison had.

"Yellowstone?" No one else had. "Okay, my thing is that I've been to Yellowstone."

Now Ethan was the only one without something. Lizzie had thought that the worst thing would be to have nothing in common with the others, but it was also terrible to have nothing about you that was distinctive. And yet Ethan was so wonderful. There had to be something special about him, some characteristic that was his alone.

Lizzie had an idea. "What's your sign?"

"My sign?"

"Your astrological sign."

"I don't know."

How could he not know? Didn't he ever read his horoscope?

"When's your birthday?"

"November sixteenth."

Lizzie stored the date in her memory for future reference. "Then you're a Scorpio. Is anyone else a Scorpio? October twenty-third through November twenty-first?"

No one was. Ethan's face brightened.

Lizzie knew there were lots of things more special about Ethan than his sign. But at least she had helped him think of something. She couldn't very well have said, "Ethan was the only one who stood up for me last year when Marcia and Alex were mean. Ethan was the one who taught me to light the bunsen burner. Ethan is the only one with a cute cowlick that sticks up on the back of his head." She accepted his smile of mingled relief and gratitude.

That was the last class Lizzie had with Ethan; he wasn't in seventh-period science or, of course, in eighth-period gym. But it would have been greedy to ask the universe for anything more.

She walked home by herself after school. The walk was long, but pleasant. As her parents were still at work, Aunt Elspeth greeted her instead. "So?" Aunt Elspeth asked. "How was it?"

"Good," Lizzie told her. "My clothes felt funny for a while, but I got some compliments from the other girls."

Two other girls besides Alison had told Lizzie they liked her top. But there had also been several groups of girls, like the three out on the blacktop, who had pointed and whispered and burst into giggles.

"Do you have anyone interesting in any of your classes?"

Lizzie loved Aunt Elspeth for understanding so well. "Yes! In three of them."

She went upstairs to change out of her jeans and tank top and into a long white dress. She was probably the only kid in her school who would change from jeans to a dress in order to feel more comfortable. Then she fixed herself a glass of lemonade, took her horoscope book, and climbed into the hammock.

One of Lizzie's many rules for herself was that she could never look at her horoscope more than one day in advance. Peeking ahead would be like reading the last page of a book first—almost like cheating.

Knowing Ethan's sign and having two horoscopes to check was exciting. She turned, somewhat nervously, to the chart in the back of the book that told which signs were romantically suited to each other. *Please, please, please, let Aries go with Scorpio.*

But Aries was matched with Leo and Capricorn. Oh, well. Many great loves had doubtless been doomed by the stars, and yet triumphed over the forces of fate.

Lizzie read Ethan's horoscope:

Scorpio (October 23–November 21). Beware of romantic attachments at this time. An old flame will try to recapture your heart. This is a good day to put business affairs in order.

Romantic attachments? Did that mean Lizzie? Was *she* an old flame? But she had never had Ethan's heart in the first place, and so could hardly "recapture" it—or had she? And "business affairs." What did they mean by "business affairs"? Maybe school? Maybe the horoscope was telling Ethan to get a good start on his schoolwork. That was clearly sensible advice.

With mounting uneasiness—how could Ethan be any further from romantic attachments than he was already?—Lizzie made herself read the entry for Aries to see what the stars held for her on the second day of seventh grade.

Aries (March 21–April 19). Be careful of appearances. Things seem to be going well, but appearances can deceive.

Once again, Lizzie was stunned by the aptness of the horoscope. How could these horoscope writers know her life so completely? *Appearances can deceive.* Yes, they *could* deceive—but did that mean they *were* deceiving? She itched to read the next day's horoscope, but made herself shut the book and keep it shut. One day at a time.

Four

On Tuesday, Lizzie put on her new green T-shirt with her jeans. She didn't even change her outfit once. And she didn't flinch as she walked into the kitchen to face her family.

Once again, Aunt Elspeth smiled at her. Once again, her father was oblivious. And once again, her mother looked worried. Not terribly worried, the way she had looked so often last year, when she was up for tenure at the university. But the lines around her eyes deepened into a tenderness that looked almost like pity. That couldn't be right. Why would Lizzie's mother feel *sorry* for her for being bold, for presenting to the world a new, improved Lizzie?

Lizzie pretended not to see. She set about making herself some cinnamon toast, grateful that the new, improved Lizzie still got to eat the same old favorite foods.

"Homework done?" her mother asked her. The question was a standing joke between them: Lizzie's homework was *always* done.

Lizzie gave her a smile. Cinnamon toast, homework joke—it was good to have some things stay the same. But even as she smiled, she wondered: Was the flawlessly done homework a problem, too, as much as the vintage clothes? Did the others resent her unbroken string of A's? Last year other kids had often called Lizzie a nerd. Were you a nerd if you got good grades? What *was* a nerd?

Well, her father was a nerd, Lizzie knew that much. She looked at him fondly, hunched over his *New York Times*, twirling his bushy beard as he read. But was her mother a nerd for loving Jane Austen and still having long, sixties-style hair, now streaked with gray? Was she, Lizzie, a nerd? How could she find out? Was there a book in the library: *Nerds: How Not to Be One*?

When her parents dropped her off at school, Lizzie slipped out of the car before anyone could see her mother kissing her. She spotted Alison, standing with a girl named Sarah who had been in Lizzie's math class last year. Shyly, she joined them.

Sarah rolled her eyes at Alison, but Alison didn't roll hers back. "Hi, Lizzie," Alison said, as friendly as she had been the day before.

"Did you get the math homework done?" Sarah asked,

speaking more to Alison than to Lizzie. "It took my parents three hours to figure it out. And my dad is good at math, too."

Lizzie hadn't thought the homework was hard. She waited to see what Alison would say.

Alison made a face. "I gave up on the last two problems. I don't think Grotient expected anyone to get them."

Lizzie had gotten them. Except for one little twist, they were just like the others.

"*You* got them all, I bet," Sarah said, turning for the first time to Lizzie. Lizzie heard open dislike in Sarah's voice, despite her new clothes.

What was Lizzie supposed to say? Was she supposed to lie? She wasn't good at lying. Pink color always flooded her face and gave her away. Sure enough, she could feel her cheeks turning warm. "I can't help it if I'm good at math," she wanted to say. But maybe she could help it. Did she really have to get every problem right, all the time?

"Well, I think I got most of them," she said cautiously.

She had to change the subject, fast. What other subjects were there? She looked at Sarah's short red skirt and Alison's white tank top, edged in eyelet lace. It was interesting that you could wear lace like that on a tank top and it was fine, but if you had a whole dress of it, you were a nerd.

"I like that top," she said to Alison.

It worked. "Do you?" Alison asked eagerly. "I wasn't sure about it."

"It's really cute," Sarah agreed. She hesitated. "I like your top, too, Lizzie," she added, as if sorry for her tone before. "That shade of green goes great with your hair."

Lizzie got the message: green top, yes; being good at math, no.

The bell rang. Day number two of Lizzie's transformation had officially begun.

As Lizzie walked into school, no one commented any further on her clothes, or did a double take when they saw her. School got off to a good start first period, when, for forty-seven happy minutes, Lizzie lost herself in the flute. It couldn't be nerdy to play an instrument. Lots of popular kids were in orchestra, though not Marcia or Alex.

In English class, Ms. Singpurwalla was wearing an orange sari. Lizzie wondered if she would wear a sari every day. Lizzie hoped so. Saris were so pretty and graceful and flowing, like Lizzie's dresses, only more colorful and exotic. Was it nerdy to wear saris? There was nothing nerdy about Ms. Singpurwalla, with her dark, gentle beauty. Maybe some people were nerds whatever they wore, while others were never nerdy, however nerdy their clothes would look on somebody else. That was an interesting hypothesis. But as Lizzie considered it, she realized it couldn't be true. She was definitely less nerdy in her new clothes. That was a plain fact.

Ms. Singpurwalla spent the first ten minutes of the class on grammar. Lizzie loved grammar, but, glancing at Marcia, she tried to mimic Marcia's bored expression as well as she could.

Then Ms. Singpurwalla told the class to get out their copies of *A Midsummer Night's Dream.* "The beauty of Shakespeare's language can be fully appreciated only if it is read aloud," she said. "Frequently, I'm going to assign parts and let you take turns on our classroom stage as young Shakespearean actors. We'll work on Act One, Scene One, today. I know the story is a little hard to follow at first. Remember, Helena is in love with Demetrius, who is in love with Hermia, who is in love with Lysander. It'll get easier as we go along. I promise! Do I have any volunteers to take a part?"

Lizzie couldn't help herself: she had to read Helena, lovesick Helena, who pined so for Demetrius. Reading over Helena's lines in Scene One last night, she had learned most of them by heart:

> *Call you me fair? that fair again unsay.*
> *Demetrius loves your fair: O happy fair!*

She *was* Helena. And Ethan was her Demetrius.

Up went her hand. At least she wasn't waving it frantically in the air. But she knew, without looking around the room, that hers was the only hand that was raised.

"Lizzie? It's Lizzie, isn't it?" That was another thing about Lizzie. Teachers always learned her name first. "What part would you like to read for us?"

"Helena," Lizzie whispered.

"Helena it is. Any other volunteers?"

To Lizzie's relief, Tom, the boy who had seen *Romeo and Juliet* at the Shakespeare festival, offered to play the part of Theseus, the Duke of Athens. She wasn't the only pathetically eager one. As Ms. Singpurwalla waited, a couple of other kids volunteered, too.

"We still need a Hermia," Ms. Singpurwalla said, once the volunteers had run out. "You . . ." She pointed to Marcia.

Marcia gave her name reluctantly.

"Marcia, you shall be our Hermia."

Lizzie saw Marcia exchange a disdainful look with Alex. Then, as always, Marcia giggled.

The cast took their places in the front of the room. The scene began. Most of the actors stumbled over the difficult lines of Shakespearean English. Ms. Singpurwalla stopped them occasionally to clarify some unfamiliar word or puzzling phrase. Lizzie noticed that Tom made a remarkably good Theseus.

Marcia read her first lines woodenly, without a single giggle. Then she reached the lines:

So will I grow, so live, so die, my lord,
Ere I will yield my virgin patent up
Unto his lordship . . .

Halfway through this speech, Marcia started laughing so uncontrollably that she couldn't continue. Unsmiling, Ms. Singpurwalla sent her back to her seat and chose another Hermia.

Helena didn't enter until late in the scene. From her opening lines, Lizzie took full possession of the part, glad she had spent so much time on it the night before. The girl who was now playing the role of Hermia breathed new life into her own lines as she spoke them in dialogue with Lizzie's Helena.

When the scene came to a close, Ms. Singpurwalla applauded, and, to Lizzie's great surprise, a few of her classmates—mostly kids who didn't know her from before—joined in. "Well done, Lizzie!" Ms. Singpurwalla said. It was wonderful to begin seventh grade with a moment of pure triumph.

But as Lizzie was leaving class, Marcia fell into step beside her. Marcia's eyes were glittering with a nasty rage. She might not have wanted to play the part of Hermia in the first place, but she plainly hadn't liked having it taken away from her.

"If *I* liked a boy," Marcia said, "I wouldn't stand up in front of the whole class and make a fool of him that way."

"What do you mean?" Lizzie asked, knowing all too well what Marcia meant.

"Did you see Ethan's face?"

Lizzie hadn't.

"How do you think he felt, with the whole class listening to you going on and on about how much you love that guy—whatever his name is—when everyone knew you were really talking about Ethan?"

Was Lizzie so obvious? She did think of Ethan as her Demetrius, but she hadn't thought Marcia would see that. Frankly, she hadn't thought Marcia would pay enough attention to what was going on in the play to figure it out. Maybe she had done *too* good a job of bringing the play to life.

"It's only a play." The defense sounded lame, even to Lizzie. "I just thought it would be fun to act it out."

"Oh, can I be Helena? Please, please, can I be Helena?"

Lizzie flushed. She hadn't waved her hand or gushed. She had taken great pains not to.

Lizzie knew right then that if she couldn't win Marcia over, she'd never fit in. She'd be Lizzie the Lizard, Lizzie the Nerd, forever.

"I didn't mean for it to sound that way," she said quietly. "Really I didn't." With one last flickering hope, born of desperation, she remembered how asking Marcia about the new clothes yesterday had worked. "Listen, if you liked a boy, what would you do?"

Marcia hesitated, as if determining whether the question was for real. "What would I do?"

The girls kept on walking. Lizzie's pulse was racing. She could feel that her cheeks were flaming scarlet. If Marcia gave her a serious answer, there was still hope. If Marcia sneered, or giggled, it was all over. At least Lizzie would be able to wear her white dresses again. But the thought held little comfort now.

"What would I do?" Marcia repeated. "Well, I certainly wouldn't write all over a huge, enormous billboard that I liked him. I'd act like I didn't like him. You know, insult him: joke insults, funny insults. Things like that."

They were at the door of the math room. There was something else that Lizzie had to ask. "If you were his PAL partner, would you help him with math?"

Marcia sighed, as if saddened that the world could contain such stupidity. But at least she answered. "I'd let *him* help *me*. Any other questions?" Her tone was sarcastic, but Lizzie had definitely heard worse from Marcia, much worse.

"No," Lizzie answered humbly. "Thanks, Marcia."

"Just use a little common sense," Marcia said. "Common sense. That's all it takes."

Common sense. Lizzie wasn't sure her common sense was the same as Marcia's common sense, but Marcia's common sense had clearly worked better than Lizzie's so far. No one could ever call Marcia a nerd, and boys liked Marcia, the same way that Demetrius and Lysander both liked Hermia. Common sense, Marcia style, might not have been recommended by Lizzie's horoscope, but Lizzie was going to give it a try.

Five

By Friday morning, Lizzie's new clothes no longer felt as foreign to her, though she still changed out of them as soon as she got home. She hadn't volunteered to read again in English class, which was fine, as Ms. Singpurwalla seemed to want to give everyone a turn. Mr. Grotient hadn't started Peer-Assisted Learning yet, which was also fine: Lizzie needed time to figure out how she could instantly become less good in math than Ethan, after years of being the class math whiz.

During first period, Lizzie half listened to the usual long list of morning announcements: the day's lunch menu, practices for field hockey and soccer, the first planning meeting for the seventh-grade dance, a back-to-school roller-skating party on Saturday night. It was time for the Labor Day weekend already: she had survived a whole entire week of seventh grade. That was good. What wasn't good was that Aunt Elspeth's visit was over: she was flying back to Chicago on Sunday.

As Lizzie started to get out her flute, Alison stopped by her chair, clarinet in hand. "Are you going to go?" Alison asked.

Lizzie had no idea what Alison was talking about: the dreaded dance was still weeks away. "Go where?" she asked cautiously.

"To the roller-skating party."

Lizzie couldn't have been more surprised if Alison had asked her, in the same casual way, if she was going up on the next space shuttle. She never went to parties; she had never been on roller skates in her life. On Saturday night she was going to a chamber music concert at the university with her parents and Aunt Elspeth.

She started to say, "No, of course not." But surely popular girls would at least consider going to parties. "I wasn't planning on it," Lizzie said guardedly.

"We could go together," Alison suggested. There was something hopeful, wistful, in her voice.

Lizzie hesitated. She wasn't used to being invited to things.

Alison apparently took Lizzie's hesitation as indecision. "Come on, Lizzie," she urged.

"I don't really know how to roller-skate," Lizzie said. It was the understatement of the century.

"Me neither!" Alison pounced joyfully on Lizzie's confession. "But if you're terrible at something, it's more fun being terrible together."

"I don't have skates."

"We can rent them there."

Things were happening too fast. Should she go? For once, Lizzie wished she had peeked ahead at her horoscope, just one day. Would Ethan go? Would Marcia laugh when she saw Lizzie trying to skate? If she refused to go, would Alison not want to be friends anymore?

"Okay," Lizzie finally said.

Alison's face lit up with grateful relief.

"Girls," Mr. Harrison interrupted them. "We're all waiting for you."

Another first for Lizzie: being reprimanded by a teacher. Hurriedly she finished assembling her flute, but she could hardly concentrate on the music. What had she gotten herself into? And could she get out of it if her horoscope indicated that this was a disastrous idea? She could always be sick: suddenly, unexpectedly, violently sick. How long did it take to come down with double pneumonia? Did people still get typhoid fever?

"About the concert tomorrow night?" Lizzie broached the subject at dinner that evening. Aunt Elspeth had made lasagna, and Lizzie wanted to savor every cheesy bite. But she couldn't enjoy eating until she had gotten her announcement over with. "Would it be all right if I didn't go?"

"Don't you want to go?" her mother asked, exchanging a look with Aunt Elspeth. It was obvious that Lizzie must have been a topic of conversation between them sometime during the past week.

"Well, I do, but there's this back-to-school roller-skating party, and I sort of promised this girl Alison I'd go with her."

"But the Tokyo Quartet—" her father began, as Lizzie had known he would.

"Of course you should go to the party," Aunt Elspeth said at the same time. "There will be other concerts." Lizzie loved Aunt Elspeth for defending her, but half wished her parents would refuse to let her miss the concert.

"Not other concerts by the Tokyo Quartet," Lizzie's father protested, but his voice was mild, as it always was.

"Is Alison a new friend?" Lizzie's mother asked. Lizzie thought there was something overly hopeful in her mother's tone, as if she was glad Lizzie had a friend at last. "Do *you* want to go to the party with her?"

"She was in French class with me last summer," Lizzie said, "and she plays the clarinet. I think I'd have more fun at the concert, but I think I *should* go to the party." At least, her horoscope thought she should—she had checked the minute she got home. For Saturday, August 30, it had said:

52

This is a good day to try something new. Romance will smile on you. Keep business affairs in the background today.

"If I don't go, Alison will have to go alone," Lizzie added.

"You don't know how to skate," her mother reminded her, as if this could possibly be something that Lizzie had forgotten.

"There's a first time for everything!" Aunt Elspeth said brightly.

This was doubtless true, but Lizzie wondered if the best time for learning to roller-skate was in front of the entire seventh grade, almost certainly including Marcia and Alex, and possibly including Ethan.

"Go," her mother said gently. "Go to the party if that's what you want."

Was it what she wanted? Lizzie didn't know.

Alison called Lizzie Saturday afternoon to finalize plans for the evening. "My mother'll drive us. We'll pick you up at seven, okay?"

"What should we wear?"

"Just regular clothes. Jeans. I'm going to wear that lacy white top. The one you said you liked. Why don't you wear the turquoise one you wore on Monday?"

Just regular clothes. Lizzie let the expression sink in.

"Okay." Lizzie paused, then said, "Alison?"

"What?"

"I can't roller-skate at *all.*"

"Then we'll hang out by the snack bar. We'll act like skating bores us." Alison laughed. "Or pretend you've twisted your ankle. You're a good actress. You can fake something."

Lizzie laughed, too. After the girls hung up, Lizzie tried to do some math homework, with limited success. She knew she'd have to double-check all the problems tomorrow, when the roller-skating ordeal would be behind her.

One nice thing had happened so far that she hadn't expected. She found herself liking Alison, really liking her, not just pretending to like her so she could fit in. She had a feeling that, in time, she and Alison might become friends.

Lizzie hung back and let Alison be the one to shyly push open the door to the rink. It was dark inside, very dark, the rink itself eerily lit by pulsating strobe lights overhead. The rock music blaring over the speakers was deafening. Lizzie had seen bumper stickers that said, IF IT'S TOO LOUD, YOU'RE TOO OLD. Twelve couldn't be all that old, but the music was way too loud for Lizzie. She couldn't help but put her hands over her ears; Alison had hers over her ears, too.

Lizzie had to shout to be heard. "Now what?"

In the dim light by the door, Lizzie could see that Alison was nervous, too. "I don't know."

"Are you girls with the West Creek Middle School group?" A teenaged girl approached them. Her red T-shirt said ROLLERAMA, so Lizzie figured she must work for the rink. "You pay over there." The girl pointed. "And then you go to that counter over there to rent your skates." As if reading their stricken faces, she added, "Cheer up. This is supposed to be fun."

By the time she sat alongside the rink, buckling on her knee pads and elbow pads, Lizzie's eyes had become more used to the darkness, and her ears somewhat more used to the noise. She had promised her parents she would rent protective equipment, though she could see that most kids didn't.

Alison strapped a helmet over her straight blond hair as Lizzie fastened one over her red curls. Lizzie couldn't imagine that she looked all that attractive and popular with her pads and helmet on. More like the goalie of a hockey team for terrified, nerdy midgets.

"Ready?" Alison shouted.

Never in a million years would Lizzie be ready for this, but she forced a fixed smile to her face and clumped behind Alison to the rink.

On the rink, Lizzie tried one tiny, tentative glide. Her skates kept going, as if bewitched by the smooth surface beneath their wheels. Just as she was about to fall, she grabbed the railing at the side of the rink and held on for dear life. Motioning with one hand for Alison to go on, she clung to the railing with the other.

Alison could skate at least a little bit, enough to let go of the railing, though she was one of the most awkward skaters there. Then Lizzie saw Marcia, whizzing by toward the center of the rink. Alex was chasing her; they were both laughing. How could their feet *go* like that, so smoothly, without making them fall?

Lizzie hobbled along the edge of the rink, relieved to discover that the railing went all the way around. It was going to be a long two hours until Alison's mother returned at nine-thirty. Right now the Tokyo Quartet would be tuning up on the brightly lit stage in a hushed auditorium. Lizzie tried not to think about it.

She was almost around the rink once when she saw catastrophe looming. The railing that was her life-support system ended at the entrance/exit to the rink, leaving about ten long feet with nothing whatsoever to hang on to. She could turn around and go back in the other direction—but everybody in the rink seemed to be going the same way, all counterclockwise, whatever their speed or proficiency. Or she could let go of the railing and try to get across that yawning gap without assistance. Or she could stand where she was for the rest of the night.

Lizzie tried the third option, since at least it allowed her to rest. Marcia and Alex sped by once, twice, three times, as Alison continued to trace a second laborious circle. Lizzie hadn't seen Ethan or Julius and hoped they weren't there yet to see her, stuck in place like a stupefied statue. On their next time past, Marcia and Alex glanced Lizzie's way and burst out laughing.

She had to make herself try option two. She could cross ten feet without a railing if she took small steps and planted her feet firmly with each one.

She took one step, then another. On the third, her feet slid out from under her and she went sprawling. How could she fall so hard when she had been going so slow? And she had no protective padding covering her tailbone.

Lizzie tried to stand up, but as soon as she awkwardly hoisted herself to her feet, down she went again, falling even harder this time. Tears of pain and humiliation stung her eyes. *This is a good day to try something new. Romance will smile on you.* As soon as she got home—if she ever got home—she was going to rip her horoscope book, every page of it, into shreds.

A strong hand reached down and grasped hers, pulling her up. It was Ethan! Quickly she blinked her tears away.

"Are you okay?" he asked.

Lizzie nodded shakily. Ethan was still holding her hand.

"Hey, Julius!" Ethan called. "Over here!" Julius appeared and took hold of Lizzie's other hand.

"Come on," Ethan said. "Hang on to us until you get used to it."

Lizzie tried to swallow the torrent of emotions that were half choking her: embarrassment, relief, gratitude, love. With a boy on each side of her, she let herself be towed slowly around the rink.

"Relax," Ethan coached her. "We've got you. You can't fall."

On their second time around, Lizzie caught sight of Alison, who was still doggedly circling on her own. Alison waved. On the third time around, Marcia passed them; she turned to stare. Then she gave Lizzie an unmistakable smile of what had to be amused congratulation.

The speakers were blaring a song Lizzie had never heard before. She could barely make out the three words: "You, me, tonight." She knew it was not what her parents were hearing from the Tokyo Quartet, but right now Lizzie preferred it to all the classical music in the world.

Then Ethan and Julius deposited Lizzie back by the entranceway.

"Thank you," she managed to whisper. She realized they couldn't hear her above the music. "Thank you!" she shouted.

"Anytime," Julius said.

Ethan gave a shy grin.

The boys skated away. Weak-legged and trembling, Lizzie eased off the rink and dropped down onto one of the benches just outside.

You, me, tonight.

Maybe she wouldn't rip up her horoscope book, after all.

Six

Lizzie slept later than usual on Sunday morning and awoke to find a bright shaft of sunlight splashed across the foot of her bed. For a few moments she lay there, soaking up the sunlight, soaking up the silence. The dark, noisy roller-skating party was over!

The five minutes Ethan had skated with her, his hand holding hers firmly—*We've got you. You can't fall*—had been the only five minutes of the party that Lizzie could honestly say she hadn't hated. Of course, they had been extremely wonderful, those five minutes. But after they were over, Lizzie had spent a long hour and a half standing by the snack bar, wishing Ethan would look her way again, waiting for the evening to end. Alison had hung out with her for most of the time, tired herself of skating, but it had been impossible to have a real conversation over the pounding, thumping bass of the music.

Her family had still been at the concert when Lizzie returned home and dragged herself upstairs gratefully to bed. So her mother and Aunt Elspeth turned expectant faces toward her when she came down to the kitchen for breakfast.

"How was it?" they said together.

Lizzie wouldn't have minded talking about the party to either of them alone, but she didn't feel like giving all the details to both of them together. For a moment she almost resented their interest in her evening. Couldn't a person go to one simple roller-skating party without having to give a full report when she returned? It wasn't that amazing that a person would go to a party, even when the person was Lizzie.

Then she relented. They only wanted to know because they loved her. And it *was* amazing that Lizzie had gone to a roller-skating party. It was.

"I didn't like it very much," Lizzie admitted. "The place was so dark, and you couldn't talk to anybody over the music, and, well, as you said, I can't skate. But I guess I'm glad I went."

She could feel her face flushing at the memory of the encounter with Ethan. She knew that Aunt Elspeth, at least, understood the meaning of the blush. It was hard having a face that told everything, even secret, private things that you wanted to treasure by yourself rather than share.

Lizzie did some more homework—yes, she had made mistakes in two of the math problems she had done yesterday in her pre-roller-skating tizzy—and read for a while: *The Mill on the Floss*, by George Eliot. Then, after a rushed lunch of leftovers, Lizzie's parents got ready to take Aunt Elspeth to the airport.

At the gate, Aunt Elspeth's eyes filled with tears when the boarding announcement came. "This has been a hard year for me." Lizzie knew Aunt Elspeth was talking about her divorce from Uncle Will. "These last two weeks have been very special."

The three of them hugged her, first Lizzie's father, then Lizzie's mother, then, last of all, Lizzie. "Thank you," Lizzie whispered. "For all the new clothes and—everything."

"You e-mail me!" Aunt Elspeth whispered back. "I want to hear more installments in the saga of how Elizabeth Bennet Archer conquers seventh grade."

As Aunt Elspeth disappeared through the gate, Lizzie wanted to call her back and tell her everything she hadn't told her: *Ethan skated with me! What do I do next?* She couldn't conquer seventh grade alone. But she was going to have to try.

The next week, it seemed as if seventh grade was going to conquer Lizzie. On Tuesday, in family living, Ms. Van Winkle led the class into a different classroom, full of sewing machines.

"Now," she said, "we are going to be learning basic sewing on the machine."

Lizzie didn't need a horoscope to predict that the sewing machines would be a complete and utter disaster. Lizzie was not good with machines. That was the main reason she couldn't ride a bike or roller-skate: bikes and skates were machines—they had wheels that moved in ways you couldn't control. Lizzie didn't even like computers. *You e-mail me*, Aunt Elspeth had said. But Lizzie preferred old-fashioned letters, written with an old-fashioned pen.

There weren't enough sewing machines for everyone in the class, so Ms. Van Winkle assigned partners: Lizzie got Julius. She was relieved. Julius was a comforting person to be with. He was kind, like Ethan, but also funny, in a cheerful, klutzy way. Last summer, when they had done French cooking in Intensive Summer Language Learning, Julius had dropped a whole pan of quiche on the floor. Lizzie had liked him ever since.

Using a diagram on the overhead projector, Ms. Van Winkle showed the class how to thread the machines. Lizzie wasn't good at diagrams. Neither was Julius. They looked at each other and shrugged helplessly.

Ms. Van Winkle circulated from machine to machine to check their work. When she got to Julius and Lizzie, she said, "No. I'm not doing it for you. Come on, you two, give it a try. Look at the diagram. The machine is just like the diagram."

Apparently Julius had been struck deaf in the last two

minutes. In any case, he didn't respond to Ms. Van Winkle's instructions. So Lizzie, with a desperate glance at the diagram, tried leading the thread around the little knobs that stuck out from the front of the sewing machine, down and up and around, like a miniature roller coaster.

"Look at the diagram again," Ms. Van Winkle said. "Help her, Julius. I want you two to figure this out yourselves."

Ms. Van Winkle went off to check on Marcia and Ethan. "Good, good," Lizzie heard her say. Had Marcia helped Ethan with it, because sewing machines were more of a girl thing? Or had Ethan helped Marcia with it, because Marcia liked to let boys feel important? Or had they figured it out together?

"Maybe it goes *under* that thing," Julius suggested.

Lizzie tried it that way. It still looked wrong.

"Maybe under that thing and over this thing?" This time Julius took his own suggestion and awkwardly redirected the thread. It still looked wrong.

"That's right," Lizzie heard Ms. Van Winkle say to Alex and Alison.

Then Ms. Van Winkle came back to check on Julius and Lizzie. "Almost," she said. "Like this." Ms. Van Winkle made some quick changes in the threading that Lizzie couldn't follow and then bustled off to check some more threading.

"Ta-dah," Julius said lamely, with a sheepish grin.

"Betsy Ross didn't have to thread a sewing machine before she made the first flag," Lizzie grumbled. "She just sewed."

Julius laughed. Ethan and Marcia looked at them curiously. Lizzie tried to think of another witty remark. But one witty remark to a boy—her first ever—would have to do for now.

On Thursday, Mr. Grotient announced the start of Peer-Assisted Learning for the new year, PAL for short. He made the same speech he had last year, about how students learned better when they learned from each other and helped each other learn.

"I've worked out your peer partners," he said then. "For those of you who had me in sixth grade, I'm keeping some of last year's partners, and others I'm mixing up."

Even though Mr. Grotient had said on the first day of school that he planned to keep successful teams together, Lizzie allowed herself to hope that this time he would put her with another girl, so she could still be as good at math as she had always been and have her help appreciated. She couldn't imagine how to follow Marcia's advice of letting Ethan help her.

But sure enough, when Mr. Grotient began to read the PAL assignments, the first names he read were Lizzie Archer and Ethan Winfield.

Maybe they could struggle together, like Lizzie and

Julius on the sewing machine. That had been fun, in a way. As Alison had said about roller-skating, if you were terrible at something, it was more fun if you were terrible at it with someone else. The only problem was that Lizzie wasn't terrible at math. She was probably the top math student in the whole seventh grade.

Last year Ethan had sat like a lump the first few times they had worked together. This time, as they shoved their desks together, he gave a small grin and said, "Here we go again."

Lizzie smiled back nervously.

They turned to the problems on page 17. Lizzie looked at the first one. The answer leaped off the page. She had found that the textbook people often made the first problem extra-easy so that everybody would understand what was going on; the problems then escalated in difficulty, with a few tricky ones at the end.

Lizzie pretended to study it. "Hmm," she said, as if perplexed. "These look hard."

As she continued to gaze down at the page, anxious not to give herself away with her usual blush, Ethan said, "Isn't the answer just $7x$ plus 3?"

It was. "How did you get that?"

Ethan shot her a suspicious look. Then, as she maintained her act of ignorance, he took a piece of paper and easily showed her.

"That looks right," Lizzie said. She copied Ethan's answer onto her own paper. "Do you do the next one the same way?" Of course you did the next one the same way. That was the whole point of the problem set. You did all the problems the same way.

Ethan picked up his pencil and stared down at the page. He looked especially cute when he was concentrating. "It's $8x$ plus 4," he finally said. "I *think* it's $8x$ plus 4."

"Oh, I get it."

There were eight more problems in the problem set. She couldn't act dumb on all of them. As Marcia would say, she needed to use some common sense. Ethan wasn't stupid, after all; if Lizzie overdid her newfound helplessness, he would notice it, if he hadn't already. So she did the next four problems with ease. Ethan did, too, Lizzie saw.

The seventh problem had a little trick to it.

"What about this one?" Lizzie asked.

She and Ethan frowned at it together—a sewing machine moment? Then Ethan shook his head. "I don't know."

Should she tell him? It was too hard not to. "Maybe if we tried it this way?" Lizzie worked it out on her scrap paper, turning the paper so that Ethan could follow her steps.

"That's it," Ethan said. Lizzie liked hearing the new note of confidence in his voice, as he pronounced authoritatively on the correctness of her answer.

Problem eight was just like problem seven. Ethan saw that on his own. Lizzie let him solve it, then copied down his answer.

Problem nine was genuinely hard. It took even Lizzie a minute to figure it out.

Ethan gave a low whistle. "Got me."

Lizzie forced herself to echo: "Me too." Her fingers itched to fly across the page with her pencil, showing Ethan how the problem was done.

Mr. Grotient stopped by their desks. "Everything all right here?" he asked in his jocular tone. "I know I don't have to worry about you two."

"Actually"—it would be even harder to fool Mr. Grotient than Ethan—"we're having some trouble with problem nine."

"Lizzie." He said her name with good-natured reproach in his tone, as if to say, *I expect better from you.* And why shouldn't he expect better? Lizzie knew the answer to nine, and to ten, too. In sixth grade she hadn't gotten a single math problem wrong all year.

Ethan gave her another quizzical look. But then, as Lizzie continued to sit silently—her misery now real, not faked—Ethan helped her out. "It doesn't solve like the others," he told Mr. Grotient.

"No, it doesn't," Mr. Grotient agreed affably.

Lizzie knew that Mr. Grotient would have helped her if she had really needed it, but she still felt annoyed at his apparent attempt to call her bluff. She refused to pick up her pencil and give in.

"Here's a hint," Mr. Grotient finally said. He wrote it on Lizzie's paper, then moved on to another pair of desks.

Worn out from pretending, Lizzie quickly solved problems nine and ten and showed the answers to Ethan.

He copied them, then said, "We did it!"

He sounded proud and pleased, as if he and Lizzie were part of a team, working together, overcoming obstacles, achieving hard-won success. Maybe Marcia's advice had been good, after all. But Lizzie's cheeks still burned with the memory of the way Mr. Grotient had looked at her when he jotted down the hint for problem nine, and then turned away.

Seven

On Friday, Ms. Singpurwalla began class by handing back their first writing assignment. It had been to take a speech from one of the characters in *A Midsummer Night's Dream* and write it over again in modern-day English. Lizzie had chosen one of Helena's speeches, of course. Actually, she had rewritten an entire scene between Helena and Demetrius at the beginning of Act Two, taking advantage of her new familiarity with the popular clique to make Shakespeare's characters sound as much like West Creek students as possible.

"I think you all did an excellent job on this," Ms. Singpurwalla said, with one of her gentle smiles. Lizzie had already taken a quick look at the grade on hers: A+. It was a grade she had come to expect on all her work, in any subject except for gym—and now, sewing machine assignments in family living—but she was still pleased.

"One of you in particular did a remarkable job, rewriting not just a single speech but an entire scene."

Lizzie's surge of satisfaction in her grade suddenly turned into a twinge of terror. She willed Ms. Singpurwalla not to say her name.

"Lizzie, would you be willing to read yours?"

Lizzie shook her head, her eyes fixed pleadingly on Ms. Singpurwalla: *Please don't make me, please don't make me, please don't make me.* But the teacher, apparently mistaking Lizzie's true desperation for false modesty, went on, "This is a scene between Helena and Demetrius."

There were some snickers in the room. By now, the end of the second week on the play, everybody knew who Helena and Demetrius were.

"Come on up front, Lizzie, and read your Helena. Who would you like as your Demetrius?"

Unable to disobey Ms. Singpurwalla, Lizzie made herself walk to the front of the room. But she wasn't going to say Ethan's name. She would die a harrowing death before his name could be forced from her lips. She expected Alex to call it out nastily—he loved teasing Ethan about Lizzie's famous crush on him. If only Ms. Singpurwalla would ask for volunteers, and Tom would raise his hand! But as Lizzie hesitated, Ms. Singpurwalla said the only name that might be even worse than Ethan's: "Alex. You can be Demetrius today."

More snickers. Clearly Lizzie was still enough of a

nerd that it was a joke on any boy to be asked to play a scene with her. And the others didn't even know yet what scene she had chosen, the scene where Shakespeare has Helena say to Demetrius:

> *I am your spaniel; and, Demetrius,*
> *The more you beat me, I will fawn on you.*

Those were the lines that Lizzie had put into modern-day English. Ms. Singpurwalla expected her to read them to wisecracking, bullying Alex Ryan in front of the entire class.

"Do I have to?" Alex asked.

"Alex." Ms. Singpurwalla's low voice had a warning in it.

Alex slouched up to the front of the room. Because there was only one copy of Lizzie's adaptation, he had to stand close to her so they could read from the same paper.

Scowling, Alex began to read:

> *I don't love you, so don't chase me.*
> *Where is Lysander and that cute Hermia?*
> *I'll kill him, but, hey, she kills me.*

The class laughed. Alex stopped and looked angry at first, but then, as if realizing that the lines he had been reading really were funny, he continued, hamming it up

72

on purpose to make his part even funnier. Lizzie felt a stirring of hope. The class was laughing with them; it wasn't laughing at them. So when she got to her longest speech, she, too, tried to bring out its comedy.

> *I'm, like, your puppy dog, and, Demetrius,*
> *If you beat me, I'll just lick your hand.*
> *Treat me like a dog, go ahead, kick me.*
> *I don't mind. Really I don't.*

The laughter in the room felt good now. When the scene was finished, the class clapped spontaneously, and Lizzie realized it was the second time in two weeks that they had clapped for her. It was the second time in her *life* that they had clapped for her.

The real question was: What would Marcia say? Lizzie didn't have to wait long to find out. At the end of class, she lingered outside the door, waiting for Marcia, to get her verdict over with.

"I didn't know you were so funny," Marcia said with appealing frankness.

"I didn't know I was funny, either."

As Alex passed by them, he gave Lizzie a grin that was almost friendly. Lizzie remembered that Alex liked being the center of attention; he was always trying to make people laugh. He must have enjoyed the applause as much as Lizzie had.

Marcia's eyes followed him. When she turned back to

Lizzie, she was still smiling, but her smile had a new edge to it. "One little piece of advice, though."

"What?"

"Stick to Ethan."

Alex's parting grin had made Marcia jealous! That was the only way Lizzie could interpret Marcia's cryptic remark. Marcia Faitak was actually jealous of her, Lizzie Archer!

But of course she would stick to Ethan. He was her Demetrius, and always would be.

At their family-living table that afternoon, before class began, Marcia asked, "Who's going to the football game tonight?"

What football game, Lizzie wondered. West Creek Middle School didn't have a football team. Lizzie knew that much about school sports.

"The high school football game," Marcia said, as if reading Lizzie's face.

All three boys were going.

"My brother Peter's on the team," Ethan said, "but he's just a freshman, so he mostly sits on the bench."

"Go, bench!" Julius cheered. "I like to root for inanimate objects," he explained.

"I've never been to a high school football game," Alison said. Lizzie didn't bother to say that she had never been, either.

"They're fun," Marcia said. "You should come. You can sit with me and Jenni and Katie." Then, as if forcing herself to spit out the words: "You too, Lizzie."

The significance of the seemingly casual invitation wasn't lost on Lizzie. She, Lizzie Archer, the Lizard, had been invited to sit with the queen of the popular girls and her court. This wasn't the kind of invitation one refused.

That evening, under a dark sky threatening snow, Lizzie found herself walking into the West Creek High School football field, with Alison by her side.

The weather was *cold*. In West Creek, Colorado, snow in September was not unheard of, and the low clouds and nippy wind certainly suggested that snow could be on its way.

"If it snows, they'll cancel the game, right?" Lizzie asked Alison hopefully.

"I don't think so. I've seen football games on TV when it was snowing. Football players are tough, you know."

Football players, maybe. But not necessarily football fans. That is, if Lizzie counted as a football fan.

They climbed to the bottom row of the bleachers, then looked around for Marcia and her friends. Lizzie couldn't see them anywhere and found herself relieved rather than disappointed.

"Let's just sit here." Lizzie gestured to a vacant

stretch of bleacher on the lowest row. She didn't like heights and was glad to sit where there was no deadly drop to the hard ground below.

Then: "Alison! Lizzie!" Marcia was waving to them from the top row of the bleachers halfway down the West Creek side.

"You go with them." Lizzie tried to make her voice light and cheery. "I'll stay here."

"Lizzie. I'm not going to leave you all by yourself. What is it?"

"I don't like heights," Lizzie admitted.

Alison gave a friendly laugh. "I'll be right next to you. And it's not like you can fall through the bleachers, or anything."

Lizzie followed Alison, first along the wide walkway at the bottom of the bleachers, then up the narrow metal steps to where Marcia and her friends were sitting. With each step Lizzie took, the bleachers seemed to shake and sway beneath her unsteady feet. What did Alison mean, you couldn't fall through the bleachers? Of course you could fall through them. Lizzie saw one boy drop something, lower himself down through the bleachers to retrieve it, and then swing himself up again. She tried not to look down as she kept on climbing.

The top row was all seventh graders. Ethan was there, and Julius and Alex, and Tom from English class, who apparently liked football as well as Shakespeare. At the sight of Ethan, Lizzie's terror of the bleachers relaxed a bit. She knew it was silly, but she felt that she couldn't fall through if Ethan was there.

She and Alison squeezed in between Marcia's friend Jenni and some boys Lizzie didn't know. Alex was right next to Marcia; Lizzie wondered how Marcia had managed that. Ethan and Julius were six or seven seats away.

Lizzie soon discovered that sitting in the bleachers was almost as bad as climbing up the bleachers. Ahead of her feet was—nothing. Behind her back was one skinny little bar, then—nothing. The void! A gust of wind rattled the bleachers. Lizzie couldn't help the small, stifled scream that escaped her.

"You're not afraid of heights, are you?" the boy next to Lizzie asked.

"A little bit."

"Look." To Lizzie's horror, he leaned all the way back, flailing his arms frantically in a pantomime of falling.

"Don't," Lizzie said.

"It's not that far down. You might break your arm, or maybe both legs, if you fell, but it probably wouldn't kill you."

Lizzie tried to ignore him and concentrate on the game, which was finally about to begin. First, though, everyone had to stand for the National Anthem. The boys next to her, clowns that they were, stood on top of their seats to get even higher. When they came to "O'er the la-and of the FREEEE!" they stamped their feet so hard that the whole bleachers shook. Even Marcia gave a squeal then and buried her face in Alex's shoulder. More than ever, Lizzie wished that she were next to Ethan.

The game began. Someone on one of the teams kicked the ball. Someone else caught it, but then a bunch of players jumped on him, and another bunch of players jumped on them, and there they all were, both teams, in this funny, writhing heap. It was so absurd, like a game played in Wonderland, that Lizzie laughed. The two boys, apparently intent on the game now, glared at her.

Lizzie swallowed her laughter and tried watching some more. The football players ran in no pattern that she could discern. A referee blew the whistle. The West Creek cheerleaders, in their skimpy little outfits, screamed, "First and ten, do it again!" The crowd joined in, but Lizzie couldn't make herself do it. She would have felt too foolish.

"Are you following the game okay?" Alison asked as the players stopped running around and falling in heaps and just stood on the field for a while, chatting.

"Not really."

"Well, it's like this. You get four downs to go ten yards. So when the cheerleaders say, 'First and ten, do it again,' that's what they're talking about. 'First' means first down, 'ten' means ten yards."

Lizzie still didn't understand. Then she thought maybe she got it. "A down, is that when they all fall down?"

"Not exactly."

All Lizzie could think of was the last lines of Ring Around the Rosy: "Ashes, ashes, We all fall down." The incongruity of the big, brawny football players dancing Ring Around the Rosy made her giggle again, but she stopped herself before the boys could give her another glare. There was probably a funny poem here somewhere, if she could think of it.

It occurred to Lizzie, with a pang of sadness, that she hadn't composed a poem since "For the Girl I Used to Be," on the first day of school. And that poem she hadn't even written down.

The wind gusted against the bleachers again. Lizzie thrust her cold hands deeper into her pockets. "How long is a game?" she asked Alison.

"There're four fifteen-minute quarters, with a break at halftime, for the marching band to play."

That wasn't too bad. Lizzie looked at her watch. Fifteen minutes had gone by already. "So we're in the second quarter now?"

Alison laughed. "No. A quarter is fifteen minutes of *playing* time, but they stop the clock between plays." She pointed toward the scoreboard. "See the clock? There's still nine minutes, twenty-three seconds left in the first quarter."

After all that running and falling and cheering and standing around, only five minutes, thirty-seven seconds had gone by?

"How long does the whole game take?"

"Oh, a couple of hours, I guess."

A couple of hours!

Lizzie invented a game of her own. She closed her eyes and counted off seconds to herself: one elephant, two elephant, three elephant . . .

Then she opened her eyes and checked how many seconds had gone by on the scoreboard clock. Once, just once, the two times matched. Otherwise, her count was off by as much as a whole minute. But it was always interesting wondering what she would find when she opened her eyes to check. Or at least more interesting than watching the game.

Suddenly, partway through one of Lizzie's closed-eye counts, she became aware that the kids all around her were on their feet, cheering, screaming, stamping.

"Touchdown!" Alison shouted to Lizzie.

Lizzie hoped this didn't mean they would stop the clock for an even longer time. But it did. Would she ever be warm again? Maybe the boys stamped their feet so much to keep them from freezing.

During halftime, most of the West Creek Middle School kids went in search of snacks at the refreshment stand. Lizzie stayed put, not eager to climb up and down the bleachers any more than she had to.

To her pleasant surprise, Ethan and Julius stopped by to say hi. "Great game!" Julius said. "Did you see that one play Peter made?"

Lizzie shook her head. Which one was Peter? All the players looked the same to her. Then she remembered: they wore different numbers.

"Which number is he?" Lizzie asked, proud that she had thought of a respectable question to ask about the game.

"Forty-three," Ethan said. He hesitated. "We're going to the snack bar. Do you want us to bring you something?"

Lizzie was touched by his thoughtfulness. "No, thanks. Alison's going to get me some hot chocolate if they have it."

"Hot chocolate sounds good," Ethan said. "It's cold, all right."

Then they went on down the bleachers.

The second half was even longer and colder than the first, if that was possible. When the final whistle blew, West Creek had won, 26 to 13. Lizzie was glad because the others were glad, but most of all she was glad that the game was over.

That night at home, lying in bed under extra covers, finally warm again, Lizzie reviewed the day. She decided there had been only four good things about that endless evening: the moment Ethan spoke to her; the moment the official clock matched her count in the clock game; the moment when she remembered, however fleetingly, what it was like to think of a poem; and the moment when the game finally ended.

Eight

In PAL math on Monday, Lizzie managed to let Ethan answer at least half the questions on his own, though she still came to his rescue for the tricky ones at the end of the problem set. She had promised herself she wouldn't help, but when the moment came to turn in an assignment with a blank for one answer and a mistake for another, she couldn't do it.

"Wait a minute," she blurted out as Ethan picked up their assignment to give it to Mr. Grotient. "I just thought of a way we might be able to do problem ten."

"How?"

Lizzie took the paper back and showed him. He looked relieved. Apparently Ethan cared about his math grade, too. Should she also tell him that the answer he had worked out for them on problem nine was wrong? He had seemed so pleased when he wrote it down. As far as Lizzie could remember, it was the first time Ethan had ever come up with his own solution to one of the trick questions. But wasn't it better that she point out the mistake to him now than that Mr. Grotient point it out to him later?

"On nine? I think maybe it's minus $7a$ plus $8b$."

Ethan studied it. "You're right." He erased his answer, rubbing too hard, so that the paper crinkled where he had rubbed. Lizzie resisted the urge to snatch the paper away from him and finish erasing it herself. Then Ethan added—ruefully, Lizzie thought—"You're always right."

"No I'm not."

"When have you ever been wrong? Name one time."

She couldn't. That was the whole problem with Lizzie: she was the smart girl, the brain, the math whiz nobody liked. But she *would* be wrong the next time they did PAL math together. It couldn't be that hard to hand in a paper with a wrong answer on it. Other people did it all the time.

On Wednesday Ms. Singpurwalla announced a class trip, in two weeks, to the rare books room at the university library.

"They have one of the nation's largest collections of Shakespeare manuscripts and memorabilia," Ms. Singpurwalla told the class. "A complete Shakespeare First Folio! That was the first collected edition of his plays—published only seven years after he died. Also, we'll be able to see, even to touch—if our hands are very clean!—

earlier manuscripts, from the fifteenth century, manuscripts that are over five hundred years old."

Although Lizzie knew the university well, from years of visiting her parents in their offices, she had never been to the rare books room. She felt gripped by the same excitement she heard in Ms. Singpurwalla's usually calm voice. To touch a piece of paper that people five centuries ago had read and loved would be a thrilling thing. Plus, Ms. Singpurwalla said they would visit the university's Shakespeare garden, filled with flowers and plants mentioned in Shakespeare's plays.

Lizzie took care not to betray her enthusiasm to anyone in the class. She was getting better at figuring out on her own what was cool and what wasn't.

Sure enough, as they were leaving class, Lizzie heard Marcia say to Alex, "A class trip to look at some musty old books in a library?"

"We're not just going to see books," Alex replied. "Didn't she say they had some rare Kleenex that Shakespeare had blown his nose on, or something?"

Marcia giggled.

For the next PAL math day, on Thursday, Lizzie's horoscope said:

Be prepared to make sacrifices today to achieve your dreams. Losses now will be offset by gains later. Look for help from unexpected quarters.

Ethan's horoscope for Thursday (she checked his every day now, too) said:

Business affairs take a turn for the worse. Be patient. Do not rely too heavily on others. Not all associates can be trusted.

Their meaning, Lizzie thought, could hardly be more obvious. She would sacrifice her perfect A in math now to win Ethan's love later. But what did they mean about help from unexpected quarters? That part didn't fit in with the rest. In Ethan's horoscope, business affairs meant math, and the turn for the worse meant that his math grade would drop just as Lizzie's did. And his grade would drop because he was relying too heavily on Lizzie. She was the associate who couldn't be trusted. That made Lizzie feel bad; it was awful to think of herself as untrustworthy.

As soon as their desks were pushed together in math, Lizzie felt her pulse racing with anxiety. It wasn't enough that she leave uncorrected a wrong answer of Ethan's; her mission was to propose a wrong answer of her own. She hoped Ethan would catch her mistake, but if he didn't, well, at least a less than perfect grade would prove that Lizzie wasn't always right.

Lizzie took turns with Ethan, offering correct answers for the first few problems. Then, on problem six, she did what she had set out to do. "I think it's $6a$ minus $2b$," she said. The correct answer was $6a$ plus $2b$.

Unhesitatingly, Ethan wrote it down. Did he trust her so much that he didn't even double-check answers she suggested?

"I *think* it's $6a$ minus $2b$." She hoped the emphasis on *think* would give Ethan the message that it might be a good idea to take another look.

Ethan stared at the problem again. "Wait," he said slowly, in a tone of disbelief. "Isn't it $6a$ *plus* $2b$?"

Lizzie felt a surge of love for Ethan as she pretended to look at number six again. "You're right. It's definitely plus."

Ethan easily changed the minus he had written to a plus. Would it be too much for Lizzie to call attention to her mistake: See? I'm *not* always right? She didn't want him to think she had been wrong on purpose. She couldn't tell if Ethan's triumph had left him feeling proud or suspicious.

Was one wrong answer enough to lose Lizzie the title of Brain? Anybody could make one careless mistake. On the next problem, Lizzie proposed another erroneous solution. This time—wiser already?—Ethan didn't write it down automatically. He seemed to think about it for a minute, but Lizzie could tell he was stumped.

"Okay," he finally agreed, and wrote the answer. Lizzie forced herself not to offer any sudden new insights into the problem. The wrong answer stared up at her reproachfully, and she went on to problem nine.

Lizzie gave the correct answer to nine, but, determined to abide by Marcia's advice and, for once and for all, get Ethan to stop thinking of her as a nerdy math whiz, she proposed another wrong answer, to ten. Ethan let it go without checking it. He appeared to accept that problem ten was beyond him.

"I'll hand it in," Ethan said. Was it a question? Was he giving Lizzie a last chance to be a math whiz forever?

"Okay."

Ethan put their paper—two wrong, 80 percent, B– — in the wire basket on Mr. Grotient's desk.

In family living, the class was still working on sewing machines. Lizzie hated them with a passion. She didn't see why sewing machines were considered part of family living. Lizzie had lived for twelve years in a family that didn't own a sewing machine. Not having a sewing machine didn't make them any less a family.

That afternoon, Lizzie was assigned to her sewing machine with Alex. It was grim to have to face her least-favorite family-living activity with her least-favorite member of her family-living family.

Ms. Van Winkle handed Lizzie and Alex each a sheet of paper printed with triangles. So far they hadn't been sewing on fabric, just on paper. Their goal was to sew around various shapes printed on pieces of paper, trying to make their line of stitching trace the shape.

"Triangle Day," Alex said glumly. "Just what I always wanted to know: how to punch a zillion tiny holes in a bunch of triangles."

For once Lizzie agreed with Alex's disparagement of a school activity. This wasn't like the remark about Shakespeare's Kleenex. Lizzie giggled. Her giggle came out sounding more like Marcia's than she had meant it to. Alex gave her a look, as if surprised that nerds could laugh, much less giggle.

"Yes," he went on, warming, as he always did, to an appreciative audience, "when I go out to get my first job, and they ask me about my skills and qualifications, I'll say, 'If you happen to have a sewing machine handy, I'll show you how I can stitch around various geometrical shapes.'"

Lizzie giggled again. Alex *was* funny sometimes. Besides, she wanted to postpone as long as possible the moment that she would have to do battle with the sewing machine.

"'Triangles, sir, are my specialty, though I'm also quite good at circles and rectangles. You don't have a job sewing triangles? Or rectangles, either? You've got to be kidding. Sewing triangles is my whole life, sir!'"

As Lizzie giggled for the third time, Ms. Van Winkle called out, "Lizzie and Alex, I don't want to hear your voices, I want to hear your sewing machine."

"She has good ears," Alex said in a low voice. "I have to give her that. Terrible lesson plans, but good hearing."

Lizzie hoped Marcia's hearing wasn't quite as good. If she hadn't liked Lizzie and Alex doing the *Midsummer* scene together, she wouldn't like them doing a sewing machine scene together, either.

To Lizzie's relief, Alex took the first turn at the machine. He positioned a corner of his triangle beneath the needle. Then he began working the machine, keeping up his comic patter the whole time. "Go baby, go! Whoa, baby, whoa! Stop. Turn. This is getting exciting now! One more corner! Take it down the home stretch. You're almost there. You're there. You went too far. Another triangle ruined, but who cares, anyway?"

Alex was acting so friendly that Lizzie leaned over to peer at his triangle. "It looks pretty good to me. All except that one little bit at the end."

"That one little bit at the end, young lady, is the difference between the triangle amateur and the triangle professional." Then, in a more normal tone, he asked, "Do you want to do one of yours, or should I keep on going?"

"Keep on going." Lizzie felt inspired to try another funny remark of her own. "I'm hoping that we'll have a fire drill today and I won't have to do mine at all."

To her astonishment, Alex laughed. Had he forgotten

that she was the Lizard, the loser, a girl no boy could ever like?

Alex kept the jokes coming as he completed three more triangles. Lizzie kept responding with appreciative giggles, till she felt almost giddy with the silliness of the afternoon. Once, Ms. Van Winkle came by to check on them, but Alex's triangles were really quite neat and accurate, so there was nothing she could say in criticism.

Too soon it was Lizzie's turn. Awkwardly she positioned her own paper in place. She poised her foot above the floor pedal, dreading the moment when the power would leap on and the needle would race forward. Her B— in math wouldn't be her first low grade of the trimester. All her sewing machine assignments so far had come back marked with C's.

Lizzie still hesitated. She couldn't make herself do it, she just couldn't.

"What's the matter?" Alex asked, not unkindly.

"I hate sewing machines. I'm not—very mechanical."

"I've noticed," Alex said dryly.

Lizzie giggled. If you were going to have to show a boy how bad you were at machines, it was better to do it with a giggle. At least, that was her working hypothesis.

"Just do it," Alex advised. "Five, four, three, two, one, ignition, blastoff!"

Lizzie touched her foot to the pedal. The machine

roared and the needle shot ahead uncontrollably, over-shooting the corner of the triangle, speeding across the middle of the adjacent triangle, racing off the edge of the page.

Then she remembered to lift her foot from the pedal. The machine stopped. Lizzie stared in despair at her ruined paper. She waited for the usual mocking remark from Alex. She deserved it, whatever it was. It was one thing to be unmechanical; it was another to be completely and irredeemably hopeless with machines.

Alex gave a low whistle. "Good thing we're not in driver's ed."

Lizzie asked Ms. Van Winkle for a new sheet of triangles. More nervous than ever, she positioned her paper for a second try. This time she bent over the paper more closely, concentrating with all her might. Again she touched the pedal; again the machine roared. Suddenly she felt a terrible tug on her scalp, which made her give a small yelp of pain as her foot jerked off the pedal.

She looked down in horror. It was true. She had sewed her hair to the page.

Alex was laughing, and Lizzie could hardly blame him. This was beyond ridiculous.

"Don't pull," he said as he leaned over and, with remarkable gentleness, eased Lizzie's hair from the tight stitching.

If only it had been Ethan.

"Thank you," Lizzie murmured.

"You really are pathetic," Alex said. But it didn't sound like the kind of thing he usually said to Lizzie.

It sounded like the kind of thing he usually said to Marcia.

Nine

Alison stopped Lizzie on the way to orchestra on Friday morning. "Do you want to go to the game tonight?"

"Sure," Lizzie said, trying to make her voice sound hearty and full of school spirit. At least this time she didn't have to ask, "What game?" This time she knew about downs, and "First and ten, do it again," and "Push 'em back, push 'em back, WAY back." She was ready.

The weather would be warmer this time, too. In fact, the day was summery, with temperatures in the upper seventies. It was hard to believe that just a week ago people had been talking about snow. Lizzie liked the unpredictability of Colorado weather. Lately her horoscope had been right more often than the weather forecast. For today it had read:

> *This is a bad day to make important decisions. Postpone them if you can. Instead, reconnect with friends and family around outdoor activities.*

Lizzie tried to think of important decisions she had to make. She couldn't come up with any: all the better. And she'd reconnect with Alison (a friend) around the football game (an outdoor activity). She should reconnect with her family, though. She hadn't spent much time with her parents lately, since she was busy with roller-skating and football games, as well as homework. She hadn't written to Aunt Elspeth, either.

After school Lizzie drifted upstairs to the two extra bedrooms that served as her parents' home offices. Both her parents usually worked at home on Fridays. Her mother's office was neat; her father's was messy. Both were lined with bookcases, overflowing with books, but her father's also had piles of books on his desk, on his couch, and on the floor. The Archers had a cleaning lady who came once a week, but she had strict instructions not to touch Lizzie's father's office.

Lizzie visited her father first. He looked up from his computer as she came in and found a place to sit amid the books and papers scattered on his lumpy, sagging sofa.

"What can I do for you?" he asked genially.

"Nothing. I'm just visiting."

He went on typing. Lizzie browsed through the papers in one of the piles; they were bristling with equations that had something to do with the nature of time. Lizzie got her math and science talent from her father.

Watching him as he worked, Lizzie was conscious

again of how different he was from other people's fathers. Alex's father, for example. Always a loud presence at school events, Mr. Ryan slapped other fathers on the back and cracked as many jokes per minute as Alex—a lot of them at Alex's expense, as Lizzie remembered. Lizzie's father disliked small talk and kidding; he didn't know what to say to people who didn't read *The New York Times*. Lizzie loved him so much, but she couldn't help hoping there wouldn't be any school events involving parents for a while, at least until her new identity was more firmly in place.

"Bye," Lizzie announced after a few more minutes of rapid-fire typing had gone by.

"You don't have to go," her father said. "You're not disturbing me."

"I know." Nothing disturbed Lizzie's father when he was writing. She sometimes wondered how her mother had ever caught his attention, back when they were in college together. What could she have said or done to make him look up from his books?

On her second visit, Lizzie found her mother on her couch, reading.

"Would you like some tea?" her mother asked. "My kettle's at the boil."

Lizzie nodded. Her mother fixed her a cup of apple cinnamon herbal tea from the kettle on the hot plate. It was a warm afternoon for tea, but Lizzie still enjoyed the first fragrant sip.

"I'm going to the football game with Alison tonight," Lizzie told her.

"Another game? You're becoming quite the fan."

"Not really. I don't watch the game, or anything. I just keep Alison company."

"I went to a few football games when I was in high school," her mother said. "I remember I worked out this little game I'd play with myself. I'd close my eyes and count the seconds, and then open my eyes and see how many seconds had gone by on the clock."

"You're kidding! That's my game! I thought it up last week."

"Like mother, like daughter," Lizzie's mother said. A little sadly? Lizzie wondered if her mother had been popular or unpopular when she was young. She had been popular enough to get married, at least. But Lizzie's mother was almost as different from the other mothers as Lizzie's father was different from the other fathers. For starters, the other mothers had shorter hair and didn't carry books with them everywhere.

"Lizzie?" her mother asked hesitantly as they continued sipping their tea. "I've been wondering. I know you think I don't like your new clothes, but I've started to get used to them. I just want to make sure that you're dressing this way because *you* want to, not because the other girls are pressuring you to look like them."

What was Lizzie supposed to say? Of course the other girls were "pressuring" her to look like them, if you called constant giggles and rolled eyes and mean comments "pressure."

"When you were my age, didn't you want to look like the other girls? Didn't you want to look normal?"

"I did," her mother admitted. "It's only that . . . looking like them is one thing, Lizzie, *being* like them is another. I think it's fine to be the new Lizzie on the outside; I just want you to be the same wonderful Lizzie on the inside."

"I am," Lizzie said shortly, though even as she said it, she knew it wasn't true. She was changing on the inside, too, into somebody who didn't write poetry, who didn't let herself be good at math, who went to football games because everybody else did, who tried to copy Marcia Faitak in all things as closely as possible.

Lizzie couldn't bear to continue the conversation. "Can I check if there's e-mail from Aunt Elspeth?"

"Go ahead," her mother said. Did she sound hurt, or was Lizzie imagining it?

Lizzie logged on to her mother's computer. There *was* an e-mail from Aunt Elspeth, a long one, full of questions about school, friends, "and anything else interesting," by which Lizzie knew Aunt Elspeth meant Ethan. But Lizzie felt funny writing back to her on e-mail. You couldn't type private things onto a bright blue screen that anybody could walk by and see.

So, curled up at the other end of her mother's couch,

still savoring her apple cinnamon tea, Lizzie wrote Aunt Elspeth a long letter on one of her mother's legal pads. She told her lots of things, but not everything. She told her about the football game, and acting out the scene from *A Midsummer Night's Dream* with Alex, and kidding around on the sewing machine with Alex. She hadn't realized she had so much to write about Alex.

Lizzie didn't write about PAL math with Ethan. She didn't think even Aunt Elspeth would understand getting a B– on purpose just to make some boy think you weren't a nerd. She knew from their conversation that her mother certainly wouldn't understand; Lizzie wasn't sure *she* understood, either.

The game was all right, though every bit as boring to Lizzie as the time before. Desperate for some diversion, she forced herself to follow Alison down the bleachers at halftime, though going down the bleachers was even more terrifying than going up. At the snack bar, she chose lemonade instead of hot chocolate to drink. It was the Kool-Aid kind, not the kind made with real lemons and sugar.

Alex had already gotten his burger and fries. "Don't you ever drink soda?" he asked.

"No," Lizzie said. Was that too strange?

"How's everything in sewing machine land?" Alex asked. "Have you sewn your hair to anything lately?"

Lizzie knew the question, though insulting, was meant to be friendly. She managed one small giggle by way of reply, followed by a blush.

"Alex." Marcia's voice was impatient. She and Alison were already heading back to the stands. Ethan and Julius were still up there; Lizzie had checked. "Are you coming or not?"

New as she was to the world of popular girls, Lizzie could tell Marcia had made a mistake. She sounded like somebody's mother. And Alex reacted as Lizzie suspected he would react to his mother: by ignoring her.

"So you don't drink soda, and you can't work a sewing machine, and you can't roller-skate, and you can't ride a bike," Alex went on, dipping a french fry in catsup. "What *do* you do?"

Lizzie tried to think of an answer. Write poetry? Too nerdy. Besides, she didn't write poetry anymore. Read? Also too nerdy. Go to classical music concerts with her parents? Off the scale for nerdiness. Stuck, she did the only thing she could think of doing: she giggled again.

"You probably can't dance, either." Now Alex was the one who looked uncomfortable, for some unaccountable reason.

Lizzie had to say something. She couldn't answer every question with a giggle. "Actually, I *can* dance, a little bit. I had two years of ballet back in elementary school."

"Like on your tippy-toes? Wearing a tutu?" Still holding his tray, Alex managed a little, effeminate twirl. "Like that?"

"Not really. I wasn't on pointe yet. I had a tutu, though."

"I bet you did. Are you going to wear it to the dance?"

The question startled Lizzie. Why would Alex be talking about the class dance, of all things, to her, of all people? "The dance?" she asked nervously.

"The seventh-grade dance? Two weeks away? Friday, September twenty-sixth? The one there're a thousand posters for all over the halls?"

Lizzie shook her head slowly. There was something unsettling about having Alex mention the dance to her, in such a shy-sounding way. "I don't have that tutu anymore. I outgrew it, and my mother gave it away."

"You? Outgrew something?"

Lizzie felt more and more awkward. The conversation had gone on too long. Everybody else had finished getting snacks and was heading back up to the stands.

"About the dance," Alex began. "You *are* going, aren't you?"

In the nick of time, Lizzie remembered: *This is a bad day to make important decisions. Postpone them if you can.*

"I haven't decided yet. The game is starting. We'd better go."

It was bad enough climbing up the bleachers. It was

worse doing it while carrying a sloshing lemonade, with Alex right behind her, so she couldn't stop every few rows to gather the courage to continue.

Finally they were back at the top bleacher. Lizzie did a quick survey of the other seventh graders. Ethan and Julius were watching the kickoff for the second half, oblivious to Lizzie and Alex. Apparently Ethan didn't know or care that Lizzie had been deep in conversation with another boy. Marcia plainly did; she looked ready to push them both off the bleachers to their deaths below.

Lizzie squeezed herself in next to Alison, glad that there was no space for Alex, who was forced to take the only open spot, next to Marcia. It was a relief not to be able to hear their conversation.

"If I didn't know better," Alison murmured to Lizzie, "I'd say that somebody likes you."

Ten

Mr. Grotient gave the problem set back to the class on Monday, when they had PAL math again. Sure enough, there was a big B– written at the top of Ethan and Lizzie's paper. Ethan stared at it in apparent disbelief.

"So what happened, you two?" Mr. Grotient asked them in a low voice. Did he know? Did Ethan know?

"The last two problems were hard," Lizzie said defensively. She knew she and Ethan weren't the only ones who had gotten them wrong.

"Let me know if you need any help on the problems today" was all Mr. Grotient said.

Lizzie looked down at the paper. Was one B– enough to make her point? Or should she get a couple of problems wrong again today?

What would Marcia do? Marcia would giggle, at least; she'd act as if she thought math was stupid and her grade was funny. Lizzie had done fairly well giggling around Alex, but she still didn't know how to giggle around Ethan. She didn't know how to talk to Ethan, either. Should she ask him what books he had been reading? Whether he was looking forward to the field trip for English? Getting bad grades together couldn't be enough to make a boy like a girl; you had to have more in common than shared failure.

For lack of any clearly better alternative, Lizzie reluctantly got to work. The first five problems were so easy she had no choice but to get them right. Then, when Ethan got the wrong answer to problem six, she let it stand. She couldn't go back to being the know-it-all nerd. She just couldn't.

Before they moved on to problem seven, she forced herself to make a real try at engaging Ethan in non-mathematical conversation. "How's Peter doing in football?" she asked, striving for a tone of casual interest. Ethan had seemed proud the other day that his brother was on the high school team.

"Weren't you at the games?" Ethan asked.

Well, that Lizzie had been *at* the games didn't mean that Lizzie had *watched* the games or could tell what any particular player had or hadn't done at the games. Should she confess her almost complete ignorance of football, accompanied by her new giggle? Maybe Ethan would feel important explaining to her all about downs and "First and ten, do it again."

Maybe not.

Sewing machines had stood her in good stead with Julius and Alex. "How do you like the sewing machines in family living?" Lizzie tried again desperately.

Ethan looked as if no one had ever asked him anything more ridiculous, which was probably true. "They're okay," he said. "What do you get for problem seven?"

Lizzie gave up and focused on the math work sheet. Doggedly, she proposed a wrong answer to problem seven, since no other technique for getting Ethan's attention seemed to work. Ethan didn't catch the mistake. Two wrong so far.

She gave the right answer to problem eight. But the answers she wrote down were wrong again to nine (Ethan's error) and ten (Lizzie's error).

Four wrong total. Bad as she was pretending to be at math, Lizzie could still figure out the percentage. 60 percent: D. She handed it in.

On Thursday, the next PAL math day, the big red D on the top of their paper looked to Lizzie as if it were red neon, pulsing with light. Her first instinct was to turn the paper facedown so no one could see it, though of course Ethan had, the one person Lizzie most wanted not to have seen it.

The rest of the papers handed out, Mr. Grotient returned to Lizzie's desk and laid his hand on her shoulder. "I'd like to talk to you after school, if you have a minute," he said.

"Okay," Lizzie said, half-miserably, half-defiantly. What could he say to her that was worse than what she was already saying to herself? She could hardly believe she had gotten a grade like that, in math, on purpose, and made Ethan get that grade, too. Maybe Mr. Grotient would e-mail her parents. She could just imagine what her mother would say; Lizzie could hardly claim this time that she was still "the same wonderful Lizzie on the inside."

Lizzie opened her math book to the new problem set. "What do you get for the first one?" she asked Ethan, trying to keep her tone as light as possible. She knew better than to make any playful inquiries about football or sewing machines.

"I don't get it," Ethan said.

"Isn't it $9x$ plus $10y$?"

Ethan pulled the book away from her and slammed it shut. "What I don't get," he said with deliberate emphasis, "is how come you're so bad at math all of a sudden."

"I told you I wasn't always right," Lizzie said in a small voice.

"Great! *I* get a D, so *you* can prove you're not always right? Is that it? What's so bad about being right, anyway?"

Didn't he know? Did he really not know? Anyway, the

D wasn't all Lizzie's fault. It wasn't as though Ethan got straight A's when he worked on his own.

"If you think you can do better, go ahead." Lizzie shoved the paper toward Ethan. Now she was angry, too.

He shoved it back to her. "You know I can't."

Mr. Grotient reappeared by their desks. "What's the matter?"

"Nothing," Ethan said sullenly.

Everything, Lizzie wanted to say.

"If I had gotten a D on my last problem set," Mr. Grotient said mildly, "I'd spend less time arguing and more time working."

When Mr. Grotient left to check on other students, Ethan went up to Mr. Grotient's desk and took a second copy of the problem set. In PAL math, they were supposed to work together and turn in one shared piece of work, but Ethan evidently was done with PAL math, or at least done with PAL math with Lizzie.

For the remainder of the period, they worked alone in silence. Ethan did all his problems himself, without looking once at Lizzie's paper. Lizzie did hers herself, too, though she couldn't resist one glance at Ethan's paper to see how he was doing. Probably a C. She gave one wrong answer on purpose, then erased it and put the right answer, then erased it again and put the wrong answer. Whatever she did, the whole thing was wrong, and she didn't know how to make it right again.

· · ·

All through the rest of her classes, Lizzie dreaded her after-school appointment with Mr. Grotient. Her spirits didn't even lift when in family living the class cut out a sewing project and didn't touch the sewing machines. She was tempted to "forget" to go see Mr. Grotient, but she knew that even if she forgot, he wouldn't. For all she knew, he had e-mailed her parents already. So at five past three, she surrendered herself at his classroom door.

"Lizzie!" he said, his greeting as friendly as if nothing had happened. "Come on in, have a seat."

Lizzie sat down. *Here it comes*, she thought.

"West Creek is forming its first math team," Mr. Grotient said, "and naturally I thought of asking you to be one of its charter members."

Lizzie was stunned. Was *this* what he had summoned her to his room to talk about? Wasn't he even going to mention the D?

"You'd train to go to a district-wide math bowl," Mr. Grotient went on. "There are regional and state-wide competitions as well. We'll practice twice a week after school, plus I'll give you some more challenging assignments to work on at home, which you're ready for anyway."

How could Lizzie be ready for more challenging assignments when she was getting near-failing grades on her regular work? She couldn't in all conscience let him go on without pointing this out.

"But—I'm not doing very well in math right now."

"That's the other thing I need to say. If you join the Mathletes, you'll be making a commitment to work your hardest for the team and to represent our school to the best of your abilities, Lizzie. This isn't about fooling around with the boys. It's about trying to learn and trying to win."

Lizzie felt herself flush, hurt at his way of putting the change in her classroom performance. Lizzie hadn't been fooling around with the boys. She had just been trying to be a normal person for once in her life.

"So what do you say, Lizzie? Can I sign you up to be on our first team of Mathletes?"

It sounded exciting and fun—it had been a long time since Lizzie remembered how much she loved, really loved, math. Mathletes also sounded like the nerdiest team in the school, maybe even in the universe. Lizzie didn't need to consult with Marcia to know that being the star of Mathletes wouldn't be like being the star of the girls' basketball team or being captain of the cheerleading squad. If she became a Mathlete, she might as well take all the new clothes Aunt Elspeth had bought her and return them to The Gap. She might as well start writing poetry again: "Ode to an Independent Variable," "Sonnet on Solving for x."

She couldn't bear to go back to being the Lizard again. Was it too much to ask just to be normal? At least sort of normal, almost normal, the next best thing to normal?

"You don't have to let me know right now," Mr. Grotient said. "I told you, this is a real commitment. You're the only one who can decide whether or not you want to make that commitment. But I hope you do, Lizzie. I don't know who started this idea that it's uncool to be smart, but in my view, what's really uncool is to throw away abilities like yours."

"I'll think about it," Lizzie said, over the lump in her throat, as she stood up to go.

"September twenty-sixth," Mr. Grotient said. "I'll need to know by September twenty-sixth. And, Lizzie, no more D's, do you hear? Or C's, or B's. Let's see those A's again."

As Lizzie hurried down the school steps, she knew she should have felt relieved. Instead of yelling at her, Mr. Grotient had offered her the ultimate compliment. So why did she feel so close to tears?

Eleven

The next football game was away. Lizzie was glad not to have to go. It was lovely to think of a whole weekend stretching ahead of her where she wouldn't have to creep up and down those unsteady bleachers, where she wouldn't have to count the seconds in her head until the game could be over.

After breakfast on Saturday, Lizzie called Alison to see if she wanted to do something else together. So far Alison had always been the one who called Lizzie: years of nerddom had made Lizzie shy about taking the initiative with other kids in social situations. But she knew it wasn't fair for Alison always to be the one to do the calling.

"Do you want to come over here, or should I go over there?" Alison asked.

"Why don't I come to your house?" Lizzie suggested, relieved that Alison had left the choice up to her. Lizzie loved her parents with all her heart, but she wasn't ready to have Alison come to her house and meet them—her father in his too-long pants, her mother in a faded dress. Maybe the next time Aunt Elspeth came to visit, she could take Lizzie's parents shopping, too.

Lizzie liked Alison's house right away. It was big, and somewhat shabby, and bursting with boys. Alison had three brothers, one older and two younger. That day the two little brothers were playing a game in which one was a lion and the other was a lion tamer. The game included lots of whip-cracking, leaping through hoops of imaginary fire, and roaring. Ten minutes into the game, all the cushions had been stripped from the couch and the coffee table was overturned.

"Maybe we should have gone to your house," Alison said, looking a bit embarrassed as Lizzie, in amazement, surveyed the wreckage strewing the lion cage. It was odd to think that Alison might be embarrassed about her family, too.

"I like it here."

"My mom's pretty much given up on peace and quiet. The only rules are: no playing with matches, no playing in the street, no climbing on the piano."

Lizzie had noticed the gleaming grand piano as soon as she had come into Alison's living room. It was the only thing in the house that wasn't battered or broken. "Do you play piano?" she asked Alison. "As well as clarinet?"

"Since I was five. It's my real instrument. I'm just doing clarinet at school for fun."

"Will you play something for me?" Lizzie had taken piano lessons herself for three years back in elementary school, before she switched to flute.

Alison shut the double doors between the living room and the family room. The sound of the roaring became muffled. Then she seated herself at the piano and played. She played beautifully. Lizzie clapped long and hard when Alison finished her piece.

"You should have brought your flute," Alison said. "We could have played duets. My mom used to play the flute, once upon a time, back when she still *had* time, and we have a bunch of sheet music duets for flute and piano."

"I'll bring it next time," Lizzie promised, certain that there would be a next time. If she and Alison both loved music, they were bound to stay friends.

The lion tamer and lion went outside, leaving the house suddenly still. There was a lull in the girls' conversation. Lizzie wanted to tell Alison about Ethan, and PAL math, and the invitation to join Mathletes, but she wasn't used to confiding in a friend, and she still felt so sick inside from her fight with Ethan on Thursday that she didn't know if she could bear putting her heartache into words.

"Let's have a snack," Alison suggested.

In the kitchen, Alison inspected the contents of the refrigerator and located a tube of chocolate chip slice-and-bake cookies. It was fun baking together. All three of Alison's brothers showed up as soon as the cookies were done, but the girls managed to save a small plateful to take up to Alison's room with glasses of milk.

"You're going to the dance, aren't you?" Alison said once they were both seated cross-legged on her bed.

"I don't think so."

"Oh, come on, Lizzie."

"What if nobody asks me to dance?"

"Are you kidding? Alex Ryan will ask you. I thought you two were going to stand there by the snack bar talking for the whole second half of the game. Julius will ask you, and I bet Tom will, too—he's like you, always so good at acting when we do the play in English class." Alison hesitated. "And Ethan."

"Not Ethan."

"He likes you. Maybe not the way you like him. But he likes you." It was the first time Alison had alluded to Lizzie's crush on Ethan.

"Not anymore," Lizzie said. Saying it out loud brought a lump to her throat. "We had a fight. On Thursday. In math class."

"What about?"

Lizzie couldn't tell her the whole story. "About some of the problems in PAL math."

"Well, that doesn't sound so serious. Listen, he's lucky he got someone as smart at math as you for his partner."

Little did Alison know how her remark stung; Ethan could hardly have felt less lucky that he had gotten the new, bad-at-math Lizzie for his partner.

"Anyway, they have girls' choice dances, too, you know. It isn't just boys asking girls. You could ask Ethan to dance. Then he'd know you want to make up. The real question is: Who's going to ask *me* to dance?"

"I think that boy who sits next to you in orchestra— Mike? I think he likes you."

Alison blushed. "What makes you think that?"

Lizzie was relieved to be talking about something other than Ethan. She knew she had lost Ethan forever—she had lost, forever, something she had never even had.

Lizzie's life had gotten desperate enough that she read ahead in the horoscope book now. For Monday, the next PAL math day, her horoscope said:

Don't rock the boat today in business affairs. Remember that slow and steady wins the race. Affairs of the heart will take a dramatic turn for the better.

Lizzie tried to focus on the one line that had caused her spirits to leap: *Affairs of the heart will take a dramatic turn for the better.* Maybe there was hope for her and Ethan, after all.

In PAL math, Lizzie wondered if Ethan would even

speak to her. Maybe he'd grab a second problem set, as he had last time, and do his work alone again. Not that she'd blame him.

"All right, PAL math today, let's get started," Mr. Grotient announced.

Before people could start shoving their desks together in the usual noisiest possible way, Ethan had his hand in the air.

"Ethan?"

"Don't you think it would be a good idea to switch PAL partners sometimes? I mean, if we're supposed to be learning from each other, wouldn't we learn more if we had lots of different people to learn from?"

Ethan had posed the question neutrally, but Lizzie's cheeks burned. Ethan was rejecting her as his PAL partner, in front of the whole class. If this was affairs of the heart taking a dramatic turn for the better, Lizzie would hate to see them take any turn for the worse.

Mr. Grotient seemed caught off guard by Ethan's question. He hesitated, then said to the class, "What do the rest of you think? Do you want to change PAL partners occasionally?"

"Change them!" Marcia called out. Lizzie knew that Marcia, who had as her PAL partner a girl named Rebecca, was hoping to get as her PAL partner a boy named Alex.

"Yeah, change them," others agreed.

Mr. Grotient sighed, as if sorry he had posed the question. "I don't want to waste a lot of time choosing people. This is a math class, not a sock hop." Marcia giggled, but Lizzie was too miserable to see any humor in Mr. Grotient's remark. How could Ethan do this? How could he?

Mr. Grotient's face brightened. "All right, count off numbers. Write your number down on a piece of paper. Your PAL partner for today will be given by this formula." He wrote it on the board, evidently pleased that he had found a way to assign the PAL partners by algebra.

Lizzie hoped that by some crazy twist of the numbers, she would get Ethan again, so she could try to make things right. If she and Ethan were assigned to each other by algebra, Ethan would have to see that it was destiny. If she didn't get Ethan, she hoped she'd get some nice, normal girl with whom she could do the math problems one-two-three without having to think about whether she was being nerdy or not—exactly what she'd wanted in the first place.

She got Marcia.

Glaring in Mr. Grotient's general direction, Marcia pulled her desk next to Lizzie's. There had been a renewed coolness between the girls since the second football game, a week ago Friday, where Alex had spent so long talking to Lizzie. Then, as if she had suddenly thought of an appropriately hurtful thing to say, Marcia's face cleared. "Too bad about Ethan," she said, her tone more smug than sympathetic.

Lizzie wished she had the nerve to reply, "Too bad about Alex." Instead, to her everlasting embarrassment, tears welled up behind her eyes.

"Oh, really." Marcia looked disgusted.

Lizzie couldn't help herself. The combination of pain and shame was too potent. She felt the first tear threatening to fall.

"Pull yourself together," Marcia hissed. "Do you want Ethan to see you crying? Act like you don't care. Act like you're having a great time without him."

Even in her misery, Lizzie noticed that Marcia's tone had changed. It wasn't gloating anymore. The advice Marcia was offering was real advice; maybe Marcia was relieved to see that Lizzie plainly hadn't switched her affections from Ethan to Alex. It was amazing to Lizzie that a girl who could be so nasty one minute could be so nice the next. Or relatively nice, at least.

Marcia giggled, a loud, staged giggle. "Oh, Lizzie! You're too much! Come on, we'd better get started on the problem set." She said the lines as if they were taken from a play, spoken by Hermia to Helena in a modern-day adaptation of *A Midsummer Night's Dream.*

"Say something," Marcia whispered imperiously to Lizzie.

Lizzie couldn't, for the life of her, think of anything to say.

Marcia kept on. "Are you crossing off the days till the class trip on Friday? Alex said we're going to see a Kleenex Shakespeare blew his nose on!" She laughed again.

Alex turned around and grinned at them, apparently enjoying having his wit in circulation. Under his gaze, Lizzie was glad Marcia hadn't let her start crying.

"Friday's the dance, too." Marcia's voice was still artificially loud. "You're going, aren't you?"

"Girls!" Mr. Grotient called to them. "None of the math problems in today's assignment has anything to do with school dances."

A lot of kids laughed then. Marcia, of course, giggled. Lizzie managed a weak smile.

Mission accomplished, Marcia dropped her act as abruptly as she had begun it. She pushed the problem set toward Lizzie. "You can do it."

Lizzie didn't want to make Marcia mad, but she had to ask, "Aren't we supposed to do it together? You're going to have to take a test on this stuff later, you know."

"Well, it's not 'later' now, is it?"

Lizzie picked up her pencil. She definitely owed Marcia a favor, and she could definitely do the problems faster alone, without having to explain every one to somebody else. But she remembered the dislike in

Sarah's voice on the second day of school, when she had been sure Lizzie had gotten all the homework problems right. Nobody liked math whizzes, girls *or* boys, except maybe for Alison. She could imagine how popular she'd be if she signed up for Mathletes.

Lizzie made herself ask the question: "Do you want me to put all right answers, or should I make some of them wrong?"

Marcia stared at Lizzie. "What do you think?"

Lizzie honestly didn't know, but she hazarded a guess. "Right answers?"

"*Duh.*"

Lizzie would never understand the rules of the popular girls' game. Quickly she answered the first five problems, delighting in the—temporary?—permission to be good at math again. But being good at math with a girl wasn't the same as being good at math with a boy. And it wasn't the same as being good at math in front of the whole school, by joining the Mathletes.

Twelve

As Friday drew nearer, all the seventh graders were talking about nothing but the dance. Lizzie overheard Marcia talking to another girl about which top to wear to the dance with which jeans, and whether Alex had said to Ethan that he thought he *was* going or that he thought he *wasn't* going. Lizzie was more interested in whatever it was Ethan had said to Alex, but that wasn't part of Marcia's report.

On Thursday, Alison and Lizzie headed outside to the picnic tables at lunch. It was finally glorious Colorado autumn weather, with cloudless skies of blazing blue.

"You still didn't tell me if you're going to the dance tomorrow," Alison reminded Lizzie.

Lizzie felt a familiar knot of dread tighten in her stomach. "I still haven't decided."

"Well, decide."

Okay, she'd decide. Her horoscope in the book had said, for Friday:

Today is a good day for mending fences. Take the initiative in reaching out to a friend who feels wronged. You won't be sorry.

That meant Ethan. She was supposed to take the initiative in reaching out to Ethan. But the horoscope didn't say how this reaching out was supposed to proceed. Or what she was supposed to do about going to the dance. Or what she was supposed to do about signing up for Mathletes.

"Okay," Alison said, since Lizzie was still fiddling with her food in silence. "I'll decide for you. You're going to the dance."

It was a relief to have one question settled. "Okay," Lizzie said. "But promise you won't abandon me if nobody asks me to dance."

"If you promise not to abandon *me* if nobody asks *me* to dance."

"It's a promise." As if Lizzie would ever be in the position of abandoning anybody for a crowd of clamoring dance partners.

Alison had answered the dance question; Lizzie might as well try her with the Mathletes question.

"Mr. Grotient is starting a math team, and he wants me to be on it." She tried to say it noncommittally, not as a question, just as a mildly interesting fact.

"That's great!" Alison's enthusiasm sounded genuine.

"Do you think I should sign up for it?"

"Why not? You're great at math, and you like it a lot, right?"

As if that was all there was to it. "You don't think it's too nerdy?"

Alison laughed. "Since when do you care about what is or isn't nerdy?"

Lizzie could tell that Alison meant the question affectionately, but the topic was too tender to Lizzie for teasing. Did Alison think Lizzie liked being a nerd? Did she really think Lizzie had been a nerd all those years on purpose? Everything Lizzie had said and done and worn for the past five weeks had been designed to end her nerddom. Hadn't it counted for anything? Was she doomed to be a nerd forever?

Lizzie stared stiffly down at her lunch.

"I didn't mean it that way." Alison laid her hand on Lizzie's arm. "That's what I like about you, that you don't care about stuff like that."

But Lizzie did care. Sometimes she felt as if she cared more than anything in the world. She forced a shaky smile for Alison and went on eating.

In family living, three of the sewing machines were out of order; Lizzie thought ruefully that if any other seventh graders were as unmechanical as she was, it was nothing short of a miracle that all the machines weren't broken.

"You'll have to work three to a machine today," Ms. Van Winkle told the class that afternoon. She read out the day's sewing machine assignments. Lizzie was to work with Alex and Ethan.

Why couldn't it have been Alison and Julius? Overcome with dread, Lizzie went to her cubby and retrieved the loathsome object that was supposed to be the makings of a tie. Both girls and boys were making ties, straight ties for the boys, wider ties for the girls, the perfect accessory to wear with clown costumes for Halloween. Sewing through fabric on the machine, Lizzie had discovered, was even harder than sewing through paper. Fabric bunched in a way that paper didn't. Lizzie's tie was already the bunchiest one in the class.

"We meet again," Alex said when Lizzie reluctantly joined the boys at their machine. "Try not to sew your hair this time, okay?"

Lizzie felt herself blushing. Alex poked Ethan in the arm. "The last time I got Lizzie, she sewed her hair to the paper," he explained, obviously waiting for Ethan to laugh.

Ethan didn't. "We'd better get started," he said, "if three of us have to have turns here."

Alex looked puzzled. Lizzie knew he wasn't used to his jokes falling flat. If only Ethan *had* laughed. For the first time she realized that worse than having someone laugh could be having someone refuse to laugh.

"Lizzie goes last," Alex said. "That way if she gets her

hair stuck in the sewing machine, at least we'll have ours done."

"Go ahead," Ethan said to Alex. Did he really have no sense of humor at all? Maybe Lizzie had made a mistake in loving him so long. At least Alex, for all his faults, was occasionally funny. At least Alex could see some humor in the world. At least Alex didn't sit glowering at her with grim-faced condemnation in his eyes. Lizzie looked away so the boys wouldn't see how close she was to tears.

"All right!" Alex said, a little too loudly, as if to make up for Ethan's and Lizzie's silence. He positioned his tie in place—one layer of the printed fabric and one layer of a stiff white fabric called interfacing. "Here goes my entry into the sewing hall of fame!"

He sewed the first seam neatly and efficiently, then the second. But when he went to remove his tie from the machine, he pretended that his head was stuck to the fabric. "Ooh! Ouch! Help, you guys! I've sewed my hair to my tie! I'm going to have to wear it as a hair ribbon now forever!"

"Cut it out," Ethan said. To Lizzie's astonishment, he sounded angry. "Leave her alone, will you?"

Alex dropped his act abruptly. "Hey," he said, "I was just kidding. It's not against the law to kid someone."

"You go next, Lizzie," Ethan said with unmistakable chivalry.

Suddenly Lizzie understood. Ethan thought Lizzie *minded* Alex's teasing; he thought she was close to tears because of Alex! Did he really not know the difference between mean teasing and flirtatious teasing? Didn't he know that Alex's teasing could never hurt Lizzie as much as his own coldness? But he wasn't acting cold now. Despite everything that had happened in PAL math, despite the D he had gotten at Lizzie's hands, he was defending Lizzie against the world once again.

Lizzie loved Ethan more than ever, not that she had ever really stopped loving him. She gave Alex a quick, apologetic smile, meant to say that *she* knew he hadn't intended to hurt her by his jokes.

And yet . . . Ethan obviously still thought of Lizzie as a loser, as a pathetic, pitiful person whom he had to protect from the Alexes of the world. He didn't seem to realize that Lizzie had changed, that Alex *liked* her now, that Alison liked her, even Marcia liked her. Everybody liked Lizzie now—except for Ethan. And Lizzie herself.

Well, she half liked her new self. She liked not being an outcast, she liked having friends, even having a real friend, Alison. She liked the new confidence she had developed; she liked being able to be funny in class, able to joke with boys. But she was worn out from trying to figure out how to be someone who wasn't good at math, someone who didn't write poetry, someone who, on the outside and the inside, was just like everybody else.

As the boys waited, Lizzie managed, for the first time, to sew her seams straight and true. But inside, everything felt more crooked and tangled than ever.

Lizzie called Aunt Elspeth after dinner, wondering if she'd be sitting home all alone or out having adventures in downtown Chicago. Aunt Elspeth answered on the third ring.

"Lizzie! How's my favorite niece?"

"Okay, I guess." Now that she had called, she didn't know exactly what it was she had wanted to say.

"Just okay? You guess?"

"I had a fight with Ethan."

"Do you want to talk about it?"

"It was about something in math class. Aunt Elspeth, do you think it's true that boys don't like girls who are good in math?"

"Not boys who are worth caring about. Do you think Ethan doesn't like you because you're good in math?"

"No." Ethan didn't like her—or liked her even less than usual—because she *wasn't* good in math, or had been acting as if she wasn't. "I just meant, in general."

"In general, I think boys—*and* girls—like people who have lots of talents and abilities, people who know who they are and who feel good about who they are."

There was an awkward silence on the phone as Lizzie let this sink in.

"Any more roller-skating parties?" Aunt Elspeth asked then.

"No. But I went to a couple of football games. And there's a dance tomorrow night."

"You're going, I take it."

"I think so."

"You're not sure?"

"Lately"—Lizzie swallowed the lump in her throat—"I'm not sure about anything."

"You know what?" Aunt Elspeth said softly. "I'm thirty years older than you are, and I'm not sure about anything, either. But I've figured out that it's all right not to be sure."

"It is?"

"So long as you don't let that keep you from trying new things. Like roller-skating parties. And dances. All kinds of new things."

And math teams? Lizzie knew that Aunt Elspeth would think she was crazy for hesitating about the math team. Aunt Elspeth wouldn't need to consult Marcia or Alison before saying yes to the math team *and* to the dance. Aunt Elspeth said yes to everything. Yet she had said no to her marriage, to staying married to Uncle Will.

"And as you try things, you'll figure out more about what you like and don't like," Aunt Elspeth went on, not seeming to mind the silence on Lizzie's end of the phone.

"And who you like and don't like. Maybe you'll make things up with Ethan. Maybe you won't. But I have a feeling it'll be okay, either way. That *you'll* be okay, either way."

Lizzie tried to hold on to Aunt Elspeth's confidence, like a rope stretched taut across the abyss of seventh grade. "I'd better go," she said, working to keep her voice from wobbling. "I have math homework due tomorrow."

Lizzie sat holding the receiver for a long moment after she hung up the phone. And then, for no reason at all, she flung herself across the bed, facedown, and broke into a passion of stormy sobs, stifling them in her soggy pillow so no one would hear.

Thirteen

On Friday morning at breakfast, Lizzie's mother was bubbling over with enthusiasm for Lizzie's class trip to the university library.

"It's been years since I've been to the rare books room, but, oh, what treasures they have! A pen owned by Walt Whitman, which he may have used to write *Leaves of Grass.* A whole entire Bible in miniature, two inches high. Gorgeous, gorgeous things."

Lizzie wanted to be excited, too. Once upon a time she would have wept with joy at the thought of being in the same room as a famous poet's actual pen. But that was before life had become so painful and complicated. Lizzie was supposed to tell Mr. Grotient that afternoon—that very afternoon—what she had decided about Mathletes. And if that weren't bad enough, that evening—that very evening—was the dance.

Even her horoscope admitted that trouble lay ahead. Lizzie had noticed that the horoscope writer tended to accentuate the positive. The horoscope never said, "Today will be an unmitigated disaster for you in every way." But for Friday, Lizzie's horoscope said:

Both business affairs and affairs of the heart require delicacy today. Avoid a slip that could be costly for both your ambitions and your affections.

How was that for a horoscope, when you were sick with nervous dread already?

As Lizzie sat poring over the horoscope at the breakfast table, her father's voice startled her. "You're not still into astrology, are you, Lizzie?"

Defensively, Lizzie laid her arm over the astrology book, as if to cover up the evidence of her fascination with the stars. "It's right an awful lot of the time."

"And it's wrong an awful lot of the time."

Was that true? Lizzie only remembered the times the horoscope had pinpointed her problems with astonishing accuracy. "I think mine's been right a lot more than it's been wrong."

"That's because people pounce on the occasional coincidence and conveniently forget the rest. Look at it this way, Lizzie. There are six billion people in the world and twelve astrological signs. Assuming that birthdays are fairly evenly distributed throughout the year, that means that half a billion people—people in Colorado, in New Jersey, in France, in Pakistan, in Peru—all share the same sign. Could there possibly be advice that would fit the needs and circumstances of half a billion different people? Here, let me see that book."

Reluctantly, Lizzie handed it to him.

He frowned at the page. "What's your sign? Aries? 'Avoid a slip that could be costly for both your ambitions and your affections.' If the slip occurs, you'll say, aha, my horoscope foretold it. If the slip doesn't occur, you'll say, aha, I managed to avoid it. Either way, the horoscope comes out looking as if it matches the truth, when in reality you're twisting the truth to make it fit."

Lizzie had to admit that what he said made sense. But seventh grade was so hard, and getting harder by the minute. She needed to feel that somehow the stars were on her side.

"I think Lizzie knows that," her mother said gently. "Horoscopes are fun to read, but Lizzie's always been someone who follows her own star."

Did her mother say it because she thought it was true, or because she wished it were true?

As her parents dropped her off in front of school, her mother gave Lizzie her usual goodbye kiss. "Have a wonderful day, my sweet Elizabeth," she said. As Lizzie reached for the door handle, she added, "Follow your star."

Lizzie's class was the only one going to the university that morning; other classes were going on other days, since the rare books room limited the size of tour groups visiting its collection. Instead of a school bus, they rode the public bus that ran by West Creek Middle School.

The bus was already crowded with people going to work, so most of the students, including Lizzie, had to stand. Lizzie was wedged in between Marcia and Ethan. Too short to reach the overhead strap, Lizzie tried to hold on to the back of the seat next to her without touching the head of the heavyset, bald man sitting there.

At the first traffic light, the bus lurched to a stop. Lizzie lost her grip on the bald man's seat and was thrown forward against Ethan. As if by instinct, Ethan reached out a hand to steady her. For the briefest of instants, his hand touched hers.

"I'm sorry," Lizzie said. She was sorry for falling against him, obviously, but also for PAL math, for embarrassing him with her crush for so many months now, for everything.

"That's okay," Ethan said. Lizzie knew he wasn't replying to her full apology. Still, he had been willing to defend her against Alex yesterday in family living. He had been willing to reach out his hand.

> *For an instant—*
> *our hands touched—*
> *Eternity—*
> *was not this much.*

The lines came unbidden into Lizzie's brain, dashes and all, like a fragment from Emily Dickinson, Lizzie's favorite poet. Lizzie didn't bother changing back into her white Emily Dickinson dresses after school anymore. She was used to jeans. They felt comfortable now. But she still loved Emily Dickinson's poetry as much as ever.

"No horsing around back there!" the driver called out, as if it was their fault that he had stopped the bus too suddenly and thrown the standees—others as well as Lizzie—off balance.

For answer, Alex gave a loud neigh. Lizzie laughed. It felt like the first time she had laughed in days.

At the university, Ms. Singpurwalla shepherded them through a stiff wind to a small, somewhat sheltered courtyard. "This is the university's Shakespeare garden." Ms. Singpurwalla gestured toward a flower bed next to a sandstone wall. "They've planted many of the flowers and herbs mentioned in various Shakespeare plays. There are a number from *A Midsummer Night's Dream.*"

Little engraved signs hung next to some of the plants. Lizzie read to herself from one of them: "I know a bank whereon the wild thyme blows." Next to her, Tom leaned over for a closer look, too.

"There's the thyme." Ms. Singpurwalla pointed to a small plant.

"Wow!" Alex exclaimed too loudly, with evident sarcasm. "Actual thyme, like you can buy in a little jar at King Soopers!"

Lizzie ignored him. She thought it was wonderful to see the thyme bush growing in this magical little garden, and to imagine Titania, the fairy queen, lying in a bed of flowers, sleeping.

"Here's another quote from the play," Ms. Singpurwalla went on. Smiling, she read, " 'Eat no onions nor garlic, for we are to utter sweet breath.' See: onion, garlic."

"Hah!" Alex breathed out loudly, right into Marcia's face. "How's that for sweet breath?" Marcia squealed and pushed him away. Lizzie was glad to see Alex paying attention to Marcia again. But then he turned to Lizzie. "Hah!" His actually not-so-sweet breath came full in her face.

"Alex," Ms. Singpurwalla said in a warning tone.

The wind came up again, and Ms. Singpurwalla hurried them into the university's massive stone library. Then she led them into the ground-floor reference room, where a librarian was waiting to give them a short tour of the library. He pointed out a large oil portrait of a stout, distinguished-looking man, after whom the library had been named.

"Hey, buddy," Alex greeted the portrait. "If you didn't hang out in the library so much, you wouldn't be so fat."

Ms. Singpurwalla shushed him, but not before some kids laughed.

As the librarian began to explain how to use the university's online catalogue, Alex made another comment, in a low voice, to Lizzie and Marcia: "Over there, by the elevator. Look at that guy with the beard!"

Lizzie looked. It was her father. He was standing in front of the elevator, an open book in his hand, reading while he waited. As was his habit when reading, he twirled one finger in his beard.

"What planet do you think he's on?" Alex continued.

Lizzie wanted to say, "Stop it. That's my father." But she couldn't say it. She wished the elevator would arrive and whisk her father, book, beard, and all, away to some other part of the library, far away from the rare books room.

Lizzie's father looked up from his book and glanced toward the tour group. He scanned them more closely, as if remembering that Lizzie's class was going to be visiting the library today. Without thinking, like a prairie dog darting into its hole, Lizzie ducked behind Alex. She couldn't bear for her father to call out to her, maybe even to come over and say hello, in front of Alex, in front of Marcia, in front of everybody. She made herself as small as she could. Finally she heard the sound of the elevator doors opening, then closing again. She was safe, for now.

Lizzie was ashamed of herself for being ashamed of her father. More than anything, she hoped her father hadn't seen her hide behind Alex. And if he had, she hoped he didn't know why she had done it. It was so easy for him, and for her mother, being different from other people. It wasn't easy for Lizzie. But lately trying *not* to be different seemed harder still.

The librarian finished his reference room presentation and led the group up the winding staircase, past the second-floor periodicals room, to the third floor. "I'll leave you now to enjoy your visit to our special collections," he said.

The rare books lady was short, almost as short as Lizzie. She flung open the door as if she were welcoming them to a holiday party at her home. "I'm Maxine. Come in, come in! We've been waiting for you!"

The class filed inside and stood in an awkward knot near the door. Maxine was so genial and friendly that Lizzie half expected her to lead them to a brimming punch bowl and a table loaded with savory, steaming treats. Instead she pointed to a different kind of feast: a table loaded with books.

"We're not going to start right away with our Shakespeare collection," Maxine said. "First I want to show you some of our other treasures, appetizers, if you will." So Maxine thought of this as a banquet, too.

"Item number one. A note written by Samuel Clemens

to himself, reminding him to pick up his laundry. Who here knows who Samuel Clemens was?"

Lizzie waited to see if anyone else would answer. Tom did: "Mark Twain."

"Yes. Now, why would we save something like this? Save it for over a hundred years? A scrap of paper with Mark Twain's little memo on it?"

"Because it's worth a lot of money?" somebody asked.

"It's probably worth quite a bit, but that's not why we save it. Why is it worth money, do you think? Why would people put such value on this?"

Alex could never resist that kind of question. Lizzie could see him trying to come up with a funny response. Unable to help herself, she blurted out, "Just *because* it's so ordinary. It makes him seem like a real person, the kind of person who has to pick up his laundry, and has to write himself a reminder to do it."

Maxine smiled at Lizzie. "Exactly!" Lizzie had made a new friend.

Marcia giggled and whispered something to Alex. Maybe it wasn't about Lizzie; maybe it was. Lizzie made her own mental memo: Don't say anything else during the rare books tour. But, oh, she was tired of having to live her life according to what Marcia Faitak would think.

The next item was an old-time typewriter, sitting next to its case, which was covered with colorful luggage stickers from various transatlantic ocean liners. It had been owned by a famous lady novelist of her time, someone Lizzie had never heard of, who had traveled around the world several times with her typewriter, pounding out novel after novel as she went. Lizzie wished people still traveled by ship and wrote with typewriters. She wished people still wrote with fountain pens.

Maxine showed them the exquisite tiny Bible Lizzie's mother had mentioned at breakfast, explaining that in the nineteenth century the Victorians had been fascinated with the making of miniature books. Even Marcia and Alex looked impressed.

"There's really a Bible in there?" Marcia asked.

"Isn't it amazing?" Maxine answered.

"What if you lost it?" Alex asked. "Like flushed it down the toilet by mistake, or something?"

"You'd have flushed away something worth forty thousand dollars, and a one-of-a-kind treasure," Maxine answered calmly.

Alex looked subdued for a moment, but only for a moment. As Maxine turned to another treasure, Alex gave an enormous sneeze into his cupped hands. Then he pretended to wipe his hands on the Mark Twain note.

In a flash Maxine whirled around and descended upon him. "I'm sorry," she said, all geniality abruptly vanishing. "We can't permit this kind of treatment of our priceless collection. I'm going to have to ask you to leave the tour."

"But I didn't do anything," Alex protested. He looked genuinely cowed by Maxine's wrath. "It was just a joke. I didn't really touch it."

"Alex," Ms. Singpurwalla said in her quiet, gentle voice. "Come with me."

"I didn't do anything," Alex repeated. "It's, like, doesn't anybody here have a sense of humor?"

"Alex."

This time Alex followed Ms. Singpurwalla out into the hallway. Through the open door of the rare books room, Lizzie saw Ms. Singpurwalla find Alex a chair. He sat down sullenly, like a small child put in time-out after a tantrum. He didn't look defiant anymore. He looked defeated.

Despite Alex's earlier remark about her father, Lizzie felt a stab of pity for him. He tried so hard to be the clown, the cutup, the life of the party. For the first time, she saw Alex with a sudden, sorrowful clarity of vision. It wasn't easy being one of the popular kids, either. Maybe having to be the person others expected you to be wasn't easy for anyone.

Lizzie focused back on the tour. "This is one of my favorites," Maxine said, gesturing toward the next exhibit, a single piece of paper covered in a peculiar round handwriting. "It's a letter written to her nephew by the poet

Emily Dickinson. I know it's hard to read, but I'll read it to you: she's included a poem in it. So we have one of Emily Dickinson's poems written in her own hand."

"Wow," Tom said to Lizzie in a low voice. "This stuff is incredible."

Lizzie couldn't even reply. She held on to the edge of the table for support as Maxine read both letter and poem. It *was* incredible that she was standing less than three feet away from a paper touched by Emily Dickinson, written on by Emily, with a poem that had flowed from Emily's pen. No typewriter for Emily. Maybe typewriters hadn't been invented then. But Lizzie knew that even if typewriters and computers *had* been invented, Emily would have written her poems by hand. Even if blue jeans and tank tops had been invented, Emily would have worn white dresses. The world had no power to stop Emily Dickinson from being Emily.

Lizzie didn't press forward to view the other exhibits. She could come back another time to see them. She lingered behind the rest, staring at Emily's poem. It wasn't even under glass. It was just *there*, on the table, as ordinary in its way as Mark Twain's note about his laundry.

Maxine interrupted the tour to say to Lizzie, "You can touch it if you want. If you're careful."

It was all Lizzie could do to make herself, let herself, touch Emily's letter. First she put out one finger and gently brought it into contact with the upper left-hand corner of the paper. She almost expected a crackle of electricity as her hand touched the paper. None came. Just a thrill so deep it made Lizzie want to cry. It made her know she'd join Mathletes and not mind what Marcia or Alex or anybody thought; it made her know that she'd write poetry again—whenever and wherever it came to her. It made her know she could be Lizzie again, at last.

Fourteen

Lizzie tried her green T-shirt with her jeans—too plain. She tried her turquoise tank top—too summery. She tried her blue sweater—too frumpy. She tried another dark green top from the Aunt Elspeth shopping trip. It was all right, but it didn't look special enough. Even though Marcia had talked about wearing jeans and a top, they didn't look like the right outfit for your first-ever school dance.

Maybe a necklace would help. Lizzie slipped her favorite locket over her head and studied the effect of the gold against the green of the top. That was a little better—but still not right. What seemed right for a dance was a dress—a long, white, flowing, feminine, old-fashioned, Emily Dickinson–style dress.

Lizzie pulled one from her closet and held it up in front of the mirror, trying it on with her eyes. She looked oddly familiar and unfamiliar at the same time, and so pretty that she hardly recognized herself. Quickly she stripped off her jeans and slipped on the dress. How could anyone think she looked like a nerd in her white dress? She looked like a girl in a long-ago story, like a girl someone would write sonnets to.

Did she dare wear it to the dance? Alison was a real friend now; she would like Lizzie whatever she wore. The Friday horoscope had made no mention of fashion, and even if it had, Lizzie didn't have to do what it said. Lizzie knew she'd keep reading her horoscope, from habit, for fun, but she was through following anybody's star but her own.

And if Marcia wanted to roll her eyes at Lizzie's return to so-called nerdiness, well, let her roll them. Nerd wasn't a thing you *were*; it was a thing other people said you were. *Nerd* was just a mean term people used when they were jealous of somebody for being smart and for daring to be different.

Lizzie's mother gave a big smile when Lizzie, a bit self-consciously, appeared downstairs dressed for the dance. "Don't you look pretty! I've missed my old-fashioned girl."

"Well, here she is," Lizzie said. Or: here she *half* was. She was an old-fashioned girl who wore a white dress sometimes and who loved poetry and who had just stopped by after school to tell Mr. Grotient that she wanted to join the math team. ("Great news, Lizzie!" Mr. Grotient had said, sounding as if he meant it.)

She was also a girl who wore jeans sometimes and who could talk to boys, who could sew on a sewing machine if she had to, and who was about to dance to rock music at a seventh-grade dance. Well, she wasn't sure about the dancing part. First of all, she didn't know how to dance, assuming that ballet didn't count; second of all, probably no one would ask her to dance, anyway.

She made a point of reaching over to give her father a quick kiss before going outside to wait for Alison.

"What's this?" he asked, but he seemed pleased. She didn't think she would have hidden behind Alex in the library if she had seen her father after she had touched Emily's letter, rather than before. In any case, she wasn't going to hide from him again, or from herself.

When Lizzie got into the backseat of Alison's mother's car, Alison said, "You look beautiful! Now I wish I had worn a dress."

In the gym, all was darkness and confusion and loud, throbbing music, the roller-skating party all over again, minus the roller skates. Lizzie realized that it didn't matter what she was wearing; it was too dark for anyone to see her, anyway. Some girls were dancing with each other. But most of the kids were standing around in awkward clumps, waiting for something to happen.

A voice came over the loudspeaker. "Girls to the north side of the gym, boys to the south." Lizzie tried to remember which side was north and which was south, but ended up just following the other girls across the gym to what was apparently the correct side.

"The first dance is boys' choice. Go to it, boys!"

Lizzie shrank behind Alison, not that she had any real fear that anybody would seek her out. From nowhere Mike appeared, the boy who sat near Alison in orchestra. He mumbled to Alison something that must have meant, "May I have this dance?" With a parting glance to Lizzie of mingled pleasure and terror, Alison followed him out to the floor.

Lizzie waited. She couldn't see any of the boys she knew. Then, across the room, still standing on the far side of the gym, she picked out a short boy who looked like Ethan and a tall boy who looked like Julius. Yes, there they were, too shy or scared or *something* to ask anyone to dance. She didn't blame them. She certainly didn't plan to ask anyone to dance when it was a girls' choice, though she thought maybe she wouldn't mind too much asking Tom. He had seemed so nice on the Shakespeare field trip, sharing her thrill in the treasures they had seen.

The music played on. No partner for Lizzie materialized from the shadows. Was it her dress, after all? The seconds passed, lengthening to minutes. Maybe she should declare defeat and call her parents for a ride home. Alison didn't need her now. She had lured Lizzie to the dance and then left her all alone, a wallflower, while *she* danced the night away with a cute boy.

Finally the music ended. Alison returned, her eyes so sparkling that Lizzie forgave her for her betrayal.

"The next dance is girls' choice," came the announcer's voice. "It's your turn now, ladies!"

Neither Alison nor Lizzie moved. "I'm going to ask him," Alison said, "but not for this dance. It's too soon."

"I'm not going to ask anyone," Lizzie said. "Ever."

"I dare you to ask Ethan."

Lizzie refused to dignify that with a reply. "Look, Marcia asked Alex."

"Surprise, surprise."

Lizzie watched them dancing together. Marcia was a good dancer, Alex less so, though infinitely better, Lizzie knew, than she herself would have been. She couldn't imagine standing out there in front of everybody, wiggling and wriggling in time to the music. If only people still danced the minuet, even the waltz. It was just as well that she was a wallflower, given that the alternative was dancing like that with a real live boy.

"Are Ethan and Julius dancing?" Lizzie made herself ask. She couldn't find them anywhere, but Alison might have better eyes.

"Julius is. Not Ethan. He's still standing by the bleachers."

Lizzie was relieved by Alison's answer.

"Do you want to go to the homecoming game tomorrow?" Alison asked. "It's on a Saturday night this week."

Lizzie contemplated a third interminable evening of

brain-numbing boredom, enlivened by a few flashes of heart-stopping terror as she climbed up and down those shaky, rickety, all-but-falling-down bleachers. "Do I have to?" she wanted to ask Alison plaintively. And just then she found herself staring face-to-face at the answer to her own question: she didn't have to.

"No," Lizzie said. Just like that. "I didn't really like the last two games very much. I don't think I'm cut out to be a football fan."

"Do you want to come over instead?" Alison asked. "Bring your flute and we'll try some duets."

Lizzie felt like flinging herself at Alison and hugging her. Instead she said, "Come to my house this time. You can bring your clarinet."

"Great," Alison said, and the music ended.

When the next dance began, a boys' choice, Lizzie composed her wallflower face to an expression of cheerful indifference to her fate. Then, suddenly, Alex stepped up to her. "Dance?"

Lizzie could hardly believe it. Alex was asking *her* to dance for a boys' choice, when he hadn't yet asked Marcia? She walked with Alex a few feet onto the dance floor. Now came the part of the evening where she would have to gyrate awkwardly to the music.

"You know how I'm bad at sewing machines?" she asked.

"No! You? Bad at sewing machines? It can't be true!"

"Well, that's how bad I am at dancing."

Alex seemed unconcerned by her confession. Rather than using it as a convenient excuse to flee back to the boys' bleachers, he said, "You said you used to do ballet. Remember, with the tutu?"

"This is the wrong music for ballet."

"You just move around. It's not like it matters what you do." Alex gave a short demonstration. Lizzie tried to imitate him. He laughed. "Don't think about it so much. Just think about the music."

Lizzie did her best, but she was relieved when the dance was over. Still, Alex had been so nice; Alex and Marcia were both surprisingly nice when Lizzie was bad at things. But if Aunt Elspeth was right, true friends would also like her when she was good at things. Alison liked Lizzie for being smart; Lizzie thought Tom might like her for being smart, too. And Ethan? He certainly hadn't liked her for acting dumb.

Lizzie waited through the next girls' choice, while Alison danced with Mike. Then Julius came to offer himself to Lizzie for a boys' choice. His klutziness was comforting. There was a good-natured goofiness to it that made Lizzie forget to care about her own awkwardness and shyness and just have fun for a change.

And for the dance after that, Tom appeared. "Miss Archer, may I have the pleasure of this dance?" he asked in a charmingly formal way. It must have been the way a gentleman in a Jane Austen novel would ask a lady to dance. Dancing with Tom was almost as enjoyable as reading Shakespeare with him in English class. If it hadn't been so hard to talk over the music, Lizzie would have asked him what he had been reading lately. She bet he would have had an interesting answer, too.

Warm now, Lizzie went with Alison to get a drink at the refreshment table. Marcia was there before them, looking uncharacteristically subdued. As far as Lizzie had seen, Alex hadn't yet asked Marcia to dance, though she had asked him on the first girls' choice. Julius and Ethan were there, too, nibbling on pretzels.

Over the loudspeaker came another announcement: "The next dance is anybody's choice. It's a slow one, so make it a good one!"

The first slow dance of the evening: a murmur of excitement and anxiety ran through the assembled girls.

Lizzie saw Alex moving toward the refreshment table. She glanced swiftly at Marcia and saw her stiffen with tense expectancy. Alex had to ask Marcia for this one, he just had to. But he walked on past Marcia, heading unmistakably toward Lizzie. This couldn't be happening: Alex Ryan selecting her for a slow dance, Lizzie the Lizard, poet, Mathlete. But it wasn't Lizzie the poet and Mathlete whom Alex liked; it was Lizzie-imitating-Marcia, the girl who giggled appreciatively at all his jokes. It wasn't the real Lizzie at all.

Lizzie had to act fast. "Ethan!" She stepped over to him before Alex could come any closer. "Will you dance with me?"

He couldn't very well refuse. He didn't say anything, but he let Lizzie lead the way out to the dance floor.

"Now what?" Ethan's tone wasn't belligerent; it was sweetly bewildered.

"You put your hand on my back, and I put my hand on your shoulder. And then our other hands go like this."

Ethan did as Lizzie said.

"And then we dance."

They danced.

It was almost enough, but not quite. "Ethan?"

"Uh-huh?"

"Are you still mad at me? About PAL math?"

For a moment Lizzie was afraid Ethan might jerk his hand away, but he didn't. "I guess not. But a D! Jeez, Lizzie. If you wanted to prove a point, couldn't you have proved it with a B?"

"That was dumb," Lizzie said. "I told you I wasn't always right about things."

"Yeah, well, I should have believed you the first time."

They swayed together to the music. A few feet away, Lizzie saw Alex dancing with Marcia, Mike dancing with Alison, Julius dancing with a pretty girl with long dark hair whom Lizzie had never seen before. Ethan's hand was warm but not sweaty, a comfortable, strong, gentle hand. Lizzie felt his other hand barely touching the small of her back. She was glad she had worn her Emily Dickinson dress to dance her first slow dance with Ethan.

Just then, the surprising truth came to her: she wasn't in love with Ethan anymore. She still liked him terribly much, and she would always cherish the memories of the times he had stood up for her over the past year. But she didn't need anyone to stand up for her now. She was standing up just fine for herself. She had a true friend; Julius, Alex, *and* Tom had all asked her to dance; she was going to give her best to the math team; she was going to write poems again, lots of them, poems that might be in the university rare books room someday.

She thought of one now, and even though she couldn't run to write it down, she knew she wouldn't forget it:

Lines Written During My First Slow Dance

> *I waited there—*
> *Upon the shelf—*
> *I reached for you—*
> *I found myself.*